STAYING IN THE GAME

Author
R.J.Red

Editorial Consultant
Halim Altinisik

Publisher

ISBN: 978-1-949872-25-5

CHAPTER 1

THE SEX PROTOCOL:

SEXTELLIGENCE

Boston

The Day of the Party

"All right! Can we get off here?" asked Inga.

"Sure," replied the cab driver.

"Thanks," said Galina, " please keep the change."

"Have fun," replied the driver.

Virginia, Langley

The Day of the Party

"Could you switch to TNT Russia, there is news about a senior bureaucrat who died of a heart attack," said Alex.

"These are normal things, now they will settle accounts within themselves and punish the mole," responded Edgar.

When Edgar tuned in on TNT Russia, it was obvious that all hell had broken loose in Moscow.

Later in the day, the news that a car had been detonated on a street close to the center of Moscow was on TV. Several top-secret service executives were also reported to have been arrested.

Despite the discomfort caused by the time difference, the CIA headquarters kept a close eye on all developments. They were really worn out having waited for the sequence of events for six days and having constantly followed the television, internet and social media for days.

After the assassination and murders in Washington D.C., the CIA and the FBI had initially sent a special warning to them, and then to the House of Representatives, Senate members and Ministers. In the letter, they were informed about the possible assassination, murder, kidnapping and assault acts that they and their family members could be faced with, so were warned to be careful.

Watching the TV intently, Edgar murmured to himself, "Well, at least they are going to fall out with each other, so their retaliation will be delayed."

Boston

The Day of the Party

Galina and Inga got out of the taxi and started to walk slowly towards the famous pub where the party was going to be held.

"Yes, here we are…"

"Nice place indeed… More elegant than it looks in the photos."

An elegantly dressed customer relations employee greeted them and asked, "Welcome. Do you have a reservation?"

"Yes, it is Anya Shervinsky."

"Our list is a bit complicated, hmm! Yes, I got it, this way please."

They walked to their table, looking around from the corner of their eyes.

Everyone was dressed in shiny tones. Just as Galina pondered on her college years, she returned to the table when a waitress suddenly said, "I can take your order if you wish." Looking at Inga, "Let's get tequila, shall we?" she asked. " Inga blinked to show her agreement.

The waitress quickly brought the tequilas. Meanwhile, the party had already begun.

Inga loved tequila with lemon and salt.

They started to take shots.

Virginia, Langley

The Day After the Party

Edgar's cell phone buzzed.

"Who is calling?" asked Alex.

"It is Senator Trasey," Edgar replied.

"The assessment of Russian sanctions will be ready in three days," he said.

Edgar nodded and picked up the phone.

"Yes, Mr. Senator."

"Mr. Edgar, I received a message on my cell phone from an unknown number. The message says, "If you don't put your son on a plane to Moscow within two days, he will die.""

"What! Did you call your son? How is he?"

"I did. He went to a party with his friend and met two girls there and came home with the girls. He is feeling sluggish with a little fever."

"Did they eat and drink anything with the girls? Did you ask it to his bodyguards as well?"

"They had a few drinks together after they met the girls."

"Who filled the glasses?"

"His friend Jack."

"Were the guards still supervising them at the time?"

"Yes, they never took their eyes off him."

"So, you're saying nothing happened at the bar, right?"

"Yes."

"They hadn't left the house for two weeks because they had been studying for final exams. Besides, the chauffeur wanted to put the bags in the trunk while the girls were getting into the car and he looked inside them. There wasn't anything remarkable in the bags, and it was electronically checked. The guard did not sense anything unusual either."

"Did the girls approach the boys by themselves?"

"No, our boys went for the girls."

"Where is your son at the moment?"

"In the villa where they spent the night."

"If you send me the address, I will get a team out there right now."

"Do not forget to send a health team as well."

"Got it."

Two Days After the Party

Paul's fever had risen to 42 Celsius.

He was quarantined in the private section of the hospital. The health teams that wore special clothes stood anxiously and helplessly by Paul's bed as they examined his test results. They were checking his body functions. The FBI and CIA agents were waiting outside the quarantine room. They asked the doctor's permission to interview Paul in order to fully understand the incident. They entered the room wearing the same special clothes and breathing masks. The interview was being recorded.

"Paul, we're from the CIA and the FBI."

"Uh-huh."

"We're trying to understand your situation."

Paul managed to half-open his eyes slowly and peered at the team of agents.

"We don't mean to worry you, but the test results show that you have been infected with a virus that has not been identified in our archives. For this reason, we want you to explain everything you experienced in the pub in detail so that we can quickly understand the situation and find a solution. Okay?"

"Got it."

"Paul, can you tell us what happened at the pub?"

"Two girls were dancing on the dance floor. Two young men went up to them and they started to talk."

"Then?"

"Then one of them grabbed one of the girls by her arm and wanted to take her away."

"Did she go?"

"No, the girl didn't want to, so he pushed her."

"What happened after that?"

"I went up to them and pushed the young man."

"What did he do?"

"'Who are you?' he said. I knocked him down with a punch."

"What happened after that?"

"The security came and of course my bodyguards…"

"Did they hit you?"

"No. They ran away as soon as they saw my bodyguards."

"Did they ever touch you or jab you with anything?"

"No."

"What did the girl tell you?"

"She said, 'You think you became a hero with one punch?"

"What did you say?"

"'Is this your way of thanking somebody?'" I said. "Her friend was next to her and she said, 'Anya is a little nervous, thank you very much.'"

"What did you say?"

"'Anya?' I said, 'What kind of name is this?!' and I burst into laughter, so did Jack."

"How did she respond?"

"'We are Polish, the Polish are not given American names,' she said."

"Then did you return to your table?"

"No, we continued to hang out together."

"What happened when you were hanging out?"

"Jack started kissing the other girl, and then I did the same with Anya."

"What happened after that?"

"After a few hours of fun, we invited the girls over to our place."

"Did they accept it?"

"Yes."

"Did you ask what they did for a living?"

"They said they both worked for an international company and pursued their master's degree at the same time."

"Well, did you see them putting something in your glasses?"

"No..."

"Sure?"

"Yes, I am. I am always careful about that..."

"What happened after that?"

"The girls went to the restroom and came back."

"And after they returned from the restroom?"

"The driver took us home."

"What did they say when they saw the driver?"

"One of them said, 'a must for alcohol nights.'"

"Can you tell us what happened when you arrived home?"

"We had sex."

"How did it start?"

"As soon as we got in, Jack took the girl into the living room and closed the door."

"I took the other girl upstairs."

"Then?"

"We had sex."

"Can you give us more details about how you started?"

"She asked for water."

"Yes."

"While fetching the water, I tripped and fell, and we laughed about it. While I was on the floor, she suddenly started to take her clothes off right in front of me."

"Did she drink the water?"

"No. The water had spilled on the floor."

"Then?"

"She started dancing in front of me."

"And then?"

"She took my hand and pulled me to bed."

"Then?"

"We started kissing each other."

"And then?"

"I got a condom from the drawer."

"Then?"

"She didn't want the condom."

"How did you know she didn't want it, what did she say?"

"She said, 'Wouldn't it be more fun if we didn't put a distance between us?'"

"What did you say?"

"I said no, I wouldn't do without it."

"What did she say?"

"'But, please' she said."

"What did you say?"

"I didn't listen. We started to make love."

"How did it start?"

"She started kissing my groins and balls. And continued with licking them."

"And then?"

"So, I moved downward licking her belly. She had a shiny, light green stone piercing in her belly."

"Did you lick her pussy?"

"No."

"Did anything get your attention? Would you please go into details as if you were living that moment, without any embarrassment?"

"Uh-huh."

It was all silent. Paul wasn't talking.

"Yes, we are listening."

"The elastic band of her underwear had left a partially visible elegant mark on her waist. Her skin was like velvet."

"..."

"And then?"

"I started licking her legs going up to her groin."

"…"

"I know you're exhausted, but keep telling me with all the strength you have left…"

"When I looked up, I saw her putting her finger in her mouth."

"Yes."

"She was sucking her fingers."

"Yes."

"Her breasts were upright. Her nipples were swollen. It was so sexy. As I was enjoying this image, she started looking at me…"

"Then?"

"She put her other hand on my shoulder and said, 'come on.'"

"Then?"

"She spread her legs."

"And then?"

"I got into her."

"Then she pushed me a bit and climbed over me."

"Were you still wearing the condom?"

"Yeah, she checked it on me with her hand, so I thought she'd take it out and I pushed her hand."

"What did she say when you did that?"

"She said, 'Relax, I just wanted to adjust it.'"

"Then?"

"We continued that way for a little while."

"Then, she said, 'Let's change it, it is not slippery anymore.'"

"What did you say?"

"I said OK."

"She reached into the closet, took the condom and opened it. She asked me to stand up."

"Then, go ahead…"

"She started licking my dick and groin again, staring at me and smiling."

"Were you still wearing the condom?"

"She had it in her hand while she was kissing my groin, then she put it on and licked my dick."

"Then?"

"She stood up and turned her back."

"Yes."

"…"

"Will you please continue?"

"She convinced me to do anal."

"Convinced?"

"I didn't want it at first."

"Would you start telling this part from the beginning?"

"She touched her ass with her hand and began stroking her hole with her middle finger."

"Yes."

"'Get in there,' she said."

"Yes."

"…"

"Could you go on with all the details? Details matter."

"I told her, 'It is very sinful according to our sect."

"She laughed lifting her neck upward. She had an indifferent attitude. Her laughter was very seductive."

"Then?"

"She said, 'It's not a sin whatsoever.'"

"And I replied, 'Whoever does this is not allowed into the heaven.'"

"Then?"

"She told me, 'This place is already like heaven, you won't need to enter heaven when you get in here.'"

"Then?"

"I did what she wanted. Then I came and we fell asleep."

"Did you sleep right away?"

"No, she threw the condoms in the water closet. Then she turned off the light."

"Did she say anything to you when you were lying down?"

"No, she slept right away."

"Well, did you sense anything different about her from other women?"

"She had a perfect ass."

"What else?"

"Very hot."

"Her ass?"

"No, all around her body."

"What else?"

"Her hip curves, size and skin were very nice."

"Did you ever feel any pain when you slept with her?"

"No."

"I mean, like her biting your lip and bleeding or sticking a very small needle?"

"No."

"If you think of a detail you didn't tell us, please share it with us."

"Sure."

Moscow

The Day After the Party

When Galina and Inga arrived at the airport, Galina's fever was quite high, and she could hardly stand.

Inga said, "Don't worry. You will feel better when you get on the plane. Hold it up a little longer." Time was dragging. Galina closed her eyes and rested her head on Inga's shoulder. Inga tried to keep Galina standing up not to draw anybody's attention and she continuously tried to chat with her.

Finally, the plane doors were opened, and they boarded. As soon as the plane took off, Galina, half dizzy, pressed the call button over their heads. She told the flight attendant in Russian, "Can I go to the restroom? I feel a little sick." The flight attendant said, "Of course, you can use the one at the back. Let me help you. You'd better hold on to the seats. Because it's dangerous to be standing while the plane is taking off."

Galina and the flight attendant headed towards the restroom.

As Galina was about to enter the restroom, the flight attendant quickly placed a pen in her hand. Galina blinked her eyes so sincerely that the flight attendant understood how important this was for Galina.

As soon as Galina locked the door, she turned the lid of the pen open and pressed the small syringe that came out into her arm without any hesitation and injected all the antidote into her blood. She got up from the toilet seat and looked into the mirror muttering herself "So, this is called love?"

"Love is a drama of contradictions."

Kafka

"You filthy Doruk, I wouldn't have done this much to Paul if I hadn't betrayed my country because of you."

"When you put the blame on others, you render yourself powerless and you lose control of your destiny."

Kirk Charles

Boston

Four Days Before the Party

When Galina and Inga landed at the airport, they were not very comfortable, but they were not anxious either. Their condition was "normal" as is often used in Russian.

The company driver had come to meet them. When Galina and Inga walked up to the driver, he threw away the colored paper on which the names of the hosting company and the guests were written and headed towards the car.

Galina had several clothes and a few pages of presentation notes printed on the letterhead paper of an international architectural company in her carry-on luggage. The two women had memorized architectural terms before leaving, and considering a contrary situation, they had studied the projects, their locations, educational details they should have learned at school to show that they had been working in the field. Everyone seemed to have studied their roles well.

Galina and Inga went up to get some rest at their hotel rooms reserved in their aliases. The rooms were adjacent to each other. As they entered, Inga told Galina, "Wake me up if you go downstairs for breakfast." Galina said, "Sure" in Polish.

The next morning, they went to the architecture company after breakfast and made their presentation. Then they came back to the hotel and fell asleep, both being wearied by travelling. The following day, they went to make their presentation at the company established by Grigory, which was not on record even in SVR.

They worked at the office until the evening for three days. When their work was done, they went out to the city for sightseeing and shopping. It was their first time in Boston, and they loved the city. While walking around, they often checked if they were being followed. There was no sign of anybody following them.

Galina could not stop thinking. Her mind lingered on the trouble that the service brought in her life, the dangerous mission that was awaiting her and having been fooled...

> *"Believing in a lie does not make you a fool because being naive is far better than being evil."*
>
> ***Victor Hugo***

She still could not accept the things that had happened. She was feeling restless inside. She thought what was done to her was contemptible and mean. "How did he do this to me?" she kept on murmuring.

When Doruk's mask slipped, she fell apart having faced the reality, and got into depression soon after. When she was faced with this fact, her feelings were as sharp as a person's feelings whose heart stopped beating while jumping down the cliff.

The truth is always an abyss."

Kafka

She could not imagine breaking up with Doruk, but his being an MIT[1] agent and befooling her had torn her heart out.

"A pair of powerful spectacles has sometimes sufficed to cure a person in love."

Nietzsche

Now she had to accept whatever happened and focus on herself. This game was no joke. If they understood that she had been working with Turks, that would mean torture to death or life sentence in prison.

"Facing the truth and adapting to it is necessary to protect oneself from external threats!"

Sigmund Freud

The heavy stress she was in was taking its toll on her stomach. Her stomach was throbbing like her heart, being destroyed by every single beat. The medication was of no use because her stomachache was due to depression.

It is the pressure on our soul that makes our body sick."

Sigmund Freud

For a moment, she thought of seeking asylum in the States. Perhaps this would be much better. Then she thought of her mother and relatives for a second. She could not do this to them. Her mom and all relatives would be jailed. There were many examples of it. Besides, they did not deserve such a thing.

She thought, "So, this is the cost of betraying one's country." This was a real and memorable lesson. It was a lesson, which might or might not be taught at the Russian Foreign Intelligence School.

"The lesson is you, but there are no students around."

Kafka

This lesson was more than enough. No matter what happened, she would never betray her country again or even think of it.

---

[1] National Intelligence Agency

"The lesson continues until you learn it."

Shaman Teaching

She thought, "Suicide might be my salvation." She had thought of suicide before joining the service. Her only wish at that moment was to give birth to a baby, and she had to live for that.

He, who has a why to live, can bear almost any how. "

Nietzsche

Galina kept thinking. "This is my only dream so far," she murmured. In fact, the only thing she wanted for herself was having a baby.

"Nothing is more your own than your dreams."

Nietzsche

Galina muttered to herself, "First of all, Doruk's real name, 'Teoman', should never cross my mind, I must forget about that name. If they happen to interrogate me, it may slip out of my mouth. Doruk must stay as Doruk in my mind."

Moscow

Eight Days Before the Party

Grigory was exhausted when his interrogation ended. The questions directed to him while he was hooked up to the polygraph had challenged him excessively. They would not let him go if they understood that he had been involved in something. Or did they leave him to find about his contacts?

Grigory just wanted to drink. As he was walking through the corridor, he had no idea whether he would ever be able to re-enter his room.

He looked around when he got to the floor of his office. There was no one. He headed towards his room. It was as if someone would appear and tell him not to enter the room until he reached out for the doorknob. He was in a weird mood.

He got in and closed the door. He grabbed a glass and filled it with whiskey. He was too depleted to put some ice into it. He felt the whiskey passing by his glands when he downed it. One thing that had occurred to him during the interrogation was that he would never be able to drink whiskey again.

He still could not make sense of how Arkady would do such a thing. Everything Arkady had said and all his life could not have been built around lies. Arkady did not deserve to be labeled as a traitor after all his services. It was impossible for him to sell himself to the CIA having had endangered his life many times for his country. Someone who hated the USA and its order could not have done such a thing. He had to prove that his assistant was not a traitor. But that was not the priority.

From the times of KGB, they had built their intelligence structure on a cellular basis. For this reason, compromising all the agents was only a possibility in case Arkady was a real traitor.

One question was bothering his mind: "If Arkady were really a CIA mole, why weren't all sleeping agents compromised and executed?" Now he had the chance to investigate this.

Grigory had to make a tough decision that had to be based on either of these two possibilities. One, Arkady was a traitor who was redesigning the USA network from scratch. Two, Arkady was a victim to a conspiracy and a senior American needed to be interrogated by employing the other sleeping agents in the USA.

Due to the distrust that was created in him because of the interrogation, Grigory could not demand an operation against a high-level American citizen such as a USA diplomat in any country but the USA.

If his demand were refused, whatever remained from his dignity would also be damaged and he would have to ask for retirement as a department head whose opinion was not heeded. Therefore, he had to make a tough decision, take control of things again and get even with the USA.

In order to get away from the events of the recent days, he went to the vineyard house called dacha. He hadn't been there for a long time. The dacha was 100 kilometers to Moscow. He left his home shy of morning.

The roads were literally empty.

When he got to the dacha, he saw that everywhere was covered with spider webs. He removed the webs using a tissue paper and sat down at the table and gazed at the clouds for some time. For the first time, he noticed the dark blue color of the clouds right before sunrise. There were many questions in his mind. He lay down on bed to get some sleep.

No sooner he had closed his eyes than the phone rang. It was Galina.

"Grigory, I'm very sorry about what happened."

"So am I."

"Where are you now?"

"In the dacha."

"You want me to come?"

"Sure."

"Okay."

"You can get the address from the center."

"Okay, see you soon."

Galina saw Grigory's car as she arrived at the dacha. She walked slowly through the gate to the door. She rang the bell. Grigory was sleeping so Galina rang the bell again. Grigory, half asleep, opened the door. Galina kissed him and said, "I am terribly sorry for what happened. I would never imagine Arkady doing such a thing."

"It's not him who did it, anyway. Did they interrogate you, too?"

"They did, but it didn't take long. Everything is about you and Arkady."

"They carried out an operation against Arkady."

"I think so, too."

"Well, who did it then?"

"CIA."

"I believe so, who else could it be?"

"Can you make some coffee? It must be in the cupboard."

"Sure, I also brought something to eat."

"Good for you, whiskey doesn't appease your hunger."

"I have pen and paper with me, just in case we need to take notes."

"We will note down things on our minds today."

"You should definitely have a plan to make the USA pay back?

"I know."

"…"

The heads of the sensitive departments such as the department of the Americans place the agents in the field unlisted and unknown even to the Director. The purpose here is to use our sleeping agents as a last resort in the event that our agents are compromised."

"…"

"We have sleeping agents of whom only I am aware."

"Great!"

Now is the time to wake those sleeping agents up. You and Inga will go to the USA immediately."

"Don't return without getting even."

"Well, do you think the payback will save Arkady?"

"The payback will not, but once he manages to pass through the stage of lie detector, injected medicine and deliberate sleep deprivation and spills out what's in his mind, it will be understood that he is not working for the CIA. Thus, he will rejoin us."

"I hope he can pull himself through this."

"Of course, if he can endure it and does not commit a suicide…"

"Do you think his physical and psychological level of tolerance is high enough?"

"It is."

Galina went back to the headquarters for the rest of the plan. She and Inga assessed the situation in the meeting room. They went through all the intelligence that came from the USA and started to make plans.

The information they obtained from student sources at the school revealed an end-of-the-year party. The date was also very close.

The families of many high-level statesmen had been briefed about security details. Security and drivers had already been designated to them.

They had to make the plan in such a way that Galina and Inga would not have to approach Senator Trasey's son, Paul; instead, they would have to make Paul come to them.

There was a lot of information about Paul in the biographic intelligence report: He always thought that he was overshadowed by his father; he was jealous of his father's power and wanted to prove himself. He rivaled his elder brother and displayed younger brother syndrome; since he was short, he had experienced the disadvantages of this physical feature at school when he was younger. For this reason, he continuously practiced martial arts and body building; despite his father's objection, he worked at a bar as a bodyguard subsequent to body building. He was fond of sex; was using Jack's social media account as he was banned from social media; he enjoyed drinking alcohol and it was even his most favorite drink.

Paul was sending friendship requests to girls through Jack's social media account using Jack's photo. Then they would meet the girl together; later, Jack would act indifferently so that Paul could start a dialogue. There was a disadvantage to using his friend's social media. No matter how indifferently Jack acted, the girls would still pick Jack several times making Paul go back to search. This was pretty much their only fun.

The statistical data about the girls whom Paul tried to communicate with from Jack's account showed that he mostly texted and sent friendship request to or liked the pictures of girls dressed in sports clothes, driving sports cars, with a slender figure, blond hair, black eyes, wearing glasses and eyeliner makeup. Information obtained from Russian students attending the same school overlapped with the typology of the girls Paul dated.

For this reason, according to their plan to attract Paul to themselves, both Galina and Inga would wear glasses, put on eyeliner and dress up in sportive clothes.

In order for Paul to notice Galina and Inga, both had to be in Paul's style and appeal to him. It might not create the desired attention if only one of them took on the type Paul preferred the most.

Paul had noticed Galina and Inga. But this alone might not have been enough for Paul to meet them. Of course, in order to attract Paul to them, someone who spoke the same language as Paul and suitable for his motives had to be found. The ground for dialogue had to be prepared. To this end, they had planned to create an incident. Creating this incident would be the responsibility of the other agents working in the company that Grigory had founded; they would act like violent men physically abusing the girls and thus Paul's attention would be attracted to the girls.

> *"If you want to communicate with a person,*
> *you should speak the language that s/he*
> *understands, not the language you know."*
>
> **Nelson Mandela**

When the event was set up and put on stage, the girls were not to immediately surrender themselves to Paul right after his intervention. As he would already be satisfied due to power display, they had to show an attitude which Paul did not expect so that his emotional state would change. This would create a sense of uncertainty and inadequacy. As a result of these feelings, Paul would have the impression that they had not surrendered, and this would eventually create some charm.

Of course, this attitude was not to be prolonged; otherwise, it could create suspicion.

The one in whom Paul was interested would inject herself with a poison in the toilet before they left the pub. This particular poison could only be transmitted through blood, causing death 72-80 hours after the infection, unless treated with its very specific antidote.

It looked like Paul was into Galina.

While Galina was making love with Paul, she opened a tiny graze on the tip of the condom using a small sharp-edged metal piece, which was placed on the pinky finger of her right hand and could be easily removed with the fingernail of the other hand.

Therefore, during the anal intercourse, the grazed condom eroded and ruptured. As a result, Galina was able to infect Paul with the poison through bleeding resulting from the deformation in the anal relationship.

"Extremity of pleasure and pain is the worst disease."

Plato

This story was also supported by the fictitious news on television. The expectation that the Russians, who fell into an internal feud, would operate very fast in the USA was forestalled. The United States was caught unprepared, just like the Russians were caught off guard when the sleeping agents of the Russians were executed. The Turks were watching what was going on in pleasure...

Greece

Ten Days Before the Party

As soon as she survived the impact of the shock and dramatic change of feelings caused by the revelation of Doruk's true identity, she began to consider whether she would share this information. If she shared it, she could be questioned too and the fact that she was working for the Turks could come to light.

Overburdened with these feelings, she quickly decided to leave the hotel and buy a new camera. She was walking very fast on the street. "Calm down," she said to herself, trying to pull herself together and being totally confused. She thought that everyone who walked by was looking at her. When she looked from the corner of her eye, she saw that people remained aloof in their own mood.

She had reached a touristic bazaar where many shops were side by side. She went into a shop that sold perfumes and cosmetic products and asked the shop owner in English, "Is there a place where I can buy a camera?" "There is a store that sells digital goods up ahead," he replied. It occurred to her that they might ask for a cell phone number for the warranty document. She silently repeated the cell phone number she had memorized before leaving the hotel.

She was walking up the street well aware of the tremor of her knees in every single step. She entered the store and looked at the cameras. "Which is the best quality camera with a reasonable price?" she asked. The shop assistant replied, "This is the most affordable one, but I would recommend that model with more memory capacity and better photo quality."

Galina held the camera and pretended to be looking at it regardless of her empty eyes. "Okay, I'll get it," she said. When she moved towards the cashier's desk, the cashier asked, "Will you pay in cash or with credit card?" Galina said "Cash," and took the money out of her purse to give it to the cashier.

The cashier asked her name, surname and phone number for the receipt. Galina said, "I'm in a bit of a hurry. If you will, you can register it in your name and it may be of use to you," and by adding "you can register it in your own name, can't you?" she made sure that the cashier adopted the idea. With the effect of the hypnotic language pattern, the cashier said, "Now that you are in a hurry, we can do that," and put the camera in a plastic bag in a desire to benefit from the promotion.

Galina asked, "Can we check if the camera is working?" The cashier replied, "Of course," carefully opening the box he said, "See? It is working, but the charge is low, so it will work 10 minutes max." Galina, with a forced smile on her face, headed for the hotel carrying the plastic bag in her hand.

As soon as she returned to her room, she turned on the camera she had bought from the elderly Greek and took pictures of all the photos in the other camera one by one. When Doruk's photo was on the screen, she threw the new camera on the floor.

She removed the memory card of the camera that was scattered around to its pieces. She quickly wiped off the machine with her clothes, thinking that fingerprints of the old Greek might be on it.

It was the biggest shock of her life. She was in a lather and both her hands and legs were shaking.

Moscow

Two Days After the Party

It could take years to find the antidote to the poison. The US officials could not afford to take the risk. When they prepared Paul and put him on a Russian plane, he was accompanied by two senior CIA officials. These officials were wearing special insulated clothing. When they landed in Moscow, the CIA liaison officer at the US Embassy in Moscow was present at the military airport. And the SVR team, of course.

While Paul was being handed over to the SVR team, The CIA officer said,

"We are not responsible for the executions in the USA. You're making a big mistake."

The SVR officials were silent.

"Paul is innocent and deserves to be delivered to our embassy after he regains his health."

SVR officials still kept silent with the dull look in their eyes.

"If we don't get Paul back, we will quickly start implementing sanctions that will result in war."

The team that took over Paul got into the minivan without uttering a single word and left the airport.

Grigory called Inga to his room and said, "We got Paul. Go and tell Galina if you want." Inga replied, "I think we should leave her alone for a few weeks until her treatment is over. Then we will inform her anyway."

Meanwhile, there was a knock on Grigory's door. The note brought to him said that a secret session was being held at the American Senate, for Paul was in the hands of the Russians. Grigory turned his head to the right and his smile lit up his face. "I think this is a new development," said Inga. Grigory explained, "Yes, it's only a matter of time before the Senators get into fight with each other. They will soon tell us their share in these events and their real purpose, thinking that similar events may happen to their own families. Of course, Arkady will turn out to be innocent. Then, we will settle the accounts inside."

The following day, although the officials in the US delegation emphasized to the SVR authorities in the meeting that the USA hadn't had any involvement or information about the assassinations, the Russians continued to believe that such an operation on US soil was not possible without the surveillance of the FBI and CIA. Their efforts to change the minds of the Russians ran into the sand.

The SVR officials asked the US officials, "In which countries did your CIA agent diplomat work before he was killed in Moscow?"

"Our murdered diplomat was not a member of the CIA. We still can't figure out why he was killed. If you have any information about this subject, we request that you share it with us."

"A fireproof-waterproof nylon diplomatic bag was found on the murdered diplomat and it had the fingerprints of a member from our service."

"What was in the bag?"

"Information on our executed personnel."

"Well then, our diplomat blew us this information while he was dead?"

"It seems that he had kept a copy of it before he died and left it at a dead drop, or had it blown to you already." The bag and the information in it might have been delivered in two copies."

"Look, our diplomat was in charge of diplomatic affairs and he had no contacts in Russia other than diplomatic relations. You must already have information about who he used to see, anyway."

"Yes, we had information, but we understand that there were points we had missed."

"Can you present any solid evidence for the alleged activities of our diplomat?"

"Some ciphered notes came out of his pocket."

"It turns out that our diplomat was exposed to a conspiracy. Maybe he was victim to a showdown in your service. We want to see any document or information other than what came out of his pocket."

"We don't have any other data."

"So, can't some other countries who are willing to get our services to confront each other have a role in this?"

"It may or may not be. We act on the basis of concrete data, not assumptions. In this case, you need to provide the data proving your conspiracy theory."

"We have some predictions."

"Which is?"

"You know ... the current structure of the UN Security Council has been opened to discussion."

"There's only one country that does not accept it, and that is Turkey."

"Turkey has only been an advocate of this issue."

"What other countries are there?"

"We haven't come here well-prepared on this issue, but we believe that there might be some efforts to disrupt the structure of the UN Security Council."

"As I said, we don't act on assumptions. The agent from whom you received the information about us has already confessed the crime."

"We do not have any information or operation regarding your executed personnel. Therefore, there is nothing to confess."

Moscow

Two Weeks Later

When Inga came to the room where Galina stayed, she told Galina, "Hi dear, you look great."

"Thanks, you too."

"Shall we go?"

"Just let me finish up writing this message."

"To your mom?"

"Yes."

As Galina didn't trust Inga, she didn't reveal that she was texting with Doruk.

When they arrived at the SVR Center, the ceremony organized to honor Galina and Inga was about to begin. Galina and Inga went to the dressing room to put on their uniforms. Both would be adorned with medals. A small crowd had been waiting for them when they arrived at the hall. The humming suddenly stopped when the SVR Director entered the hall.

After the national anthem and a moment of silence, the SVR Director was invited to the podium. As the director walked slowly to the podium, the hall was dead silent again.

The SVR Director glanced at the hall from the podium and began to speak:

"Our country is confronted with ever-complicated events and new multidimensional attacks every day. We have to equip ourselves with new skills, new knowledge and equipment every single day. The world has now accepted the power of the Russian Federation. Maps of our country divided, which was shared in the media in the past years, are no longer included in the printed and visual media. Our success in intelligence gathering, evaluation and operation is getting much better every day."

The crowd, who applauded the director on the cue of the director's pause for taking a breath, resumed listening to him attentively.

"We will invite our heroes to the stage again on this meaningful day. Our country continues to produce heroes and heroines under any circumstances regardless of the cost. I would like to invite our heroines, whose names will be ardently engraved in the history, to present their medals and wish them continued success."

The Director continued his speech by looking at the paper.

"Galina Ivanova and Inga Sokolova."

Galina's and Inga's faces registered their excitement evidently. The director presented their medals on a plaque after warmly shaking hands. As Galina and Inga were staring at their medals, their pride could easily be seen in their eyes.

The medals were not delivered to Galina and Inga for security reasons and were moved to the SVR archives.

While everyone was sipping their drinks, which accompanied caviar served on toasted bread, Grigory saw the Director and his deputies by the door, then walked over to Galina. Galina asked Grigory, "Has Paul pulled himself together?"

"Yes."

"When are you going to send Paul back?"

"Two days later."

"Can I get him to the airport?"

"No..."

"In exchange of what will they release Paul?"

"It hasn't been concluded exactly whether the Americans did this operation, as usual. And the Americans did not accept it in any way."

"They couldn't be expected to accept it anyway."

"Sometimes they do accept."

"So, they weren't in such a difficult situation."

"I guess so. We asked for the execution of an equal number of people and gave the list. Although they are all under American protection, they will be killed the same day. News and supporting CCTV footage - side buildings, roads, etc.- of the executions will be distributed to the press. Our revenge will be announced to the world publicly. Of course, we will have observers in the executions. We can't trust the Americans," he said.

"I wish we had wanted twice as many."

"I wish, too."

"So, why didn't we ask for agents from their sleeping agents list?"

"Instead of giving the right people, they could have given ordinary people or the people they wanted to be eliminated."

"Yes."

"That's why we didn't take a chance by giving our own list. The world public is already familiar with the three people who we want to be executed. Among them are oligarchs and activists who sought asylum from the United States."

"The list is great then; it will be easily understood that it is a revenge."

"Absolutely."

"Meanwhile, our source in Turkey requests a meet."

"Make a plan and meet with him but be very careful."

After this dialogue, she left Grigory and walked towards the table where Inga was sitting. Galina had survived the effect of the poison, but still suffered minor dizziness while standing. Inga said, "We received the award but did not discuss the path leading to the award. Tell me what happened that night."

"I will tell you later, but you will tell me too," said Galina.

Inga smiled, "Deal!"

CHAPTER 2

AGREEING TO SPEAK

Galina hadn't met Olga for a long time. She was her best friend and confidant. But there were certain things she could not talk even with her. Still, she wanted to open up to her somehow. She was obsessed with what Doruk had done to her and was not able to sleep at nights. She decided to call Olga and wanted to visit her. Olga was so glad, and they set a date.

When Galina went to Olga's place, she immediately noticed that the wallpapers had changed. She got used to it very much when she lived in Olga's house. When they started to chat, she told Olga that she was going through tough days with many problems and didn't know what to do to get rid of them.

"If you can give me some details, maybe we can find a solution or if you want, let's make an appointment with Ms. Yulya again."

"I can't tell Yulya what happened to me. But may I ask you to do me a favor? It might work better for me."

"Sure, go ahead."

"But it is something strange."

"Gala, you know I'd do anything for you, come on, tell me."

"..."

"Come on, Gala."

"I have not been impressed by many words or quotes. Once though, when I went to Azerbaijan for a job, I entered a bookstore to spend some time. I went through books and came across a sentence which I mocked saying, 'Oh, what the heck?' But then I ran into that sentence at the most important point of my life."

"Do you remember the name of the book?"

"No."

"So, what do you want me to do?"

"Can you go to that bookstore in Baku and bring me some books if I pay all travel costs?"

"I will, but how will I know that I choose the right book?"

"Think of me in your heart as you are entering the bookstore and you will come across it."

"How many books should I buy then?"

"You can get as many as you wish."

"Okay, tomorrow I'm going to take the day off and go as soon as I can."

"Does the language matter?"

"It had better be in Russian. But I also understand Azerbaijani Turkish, since I know Turkish."

"Got it."

"You should see around for a few days while you're there, so you won't get tired with travelling."

"No, I can't do that while you're so desperate, I'll just go and come back in no time. Later we can go there and walk around together."

"So, do you remember what kind of books you were looking at? How was its cover page?"

"It was like a novel, there were quotations in it."

"You hope the quotations in the book will guide you, right?"

"Yes, that's true, I hope they do. The quotations were written in bold letters."

"Is there anything else you want except for the book?"

"No, thanks."

Back from Baku

"Hello."

"Hello dear."

"How was the journey?"

"It was good, and it's been a change for me."

"Come on in."

"..."

"Are the shoes new?"

"I got them from America."

"Very stylish."

"Care for some coffee?"

"Wait, let's get it together."

"I'll bring you right away with my phone."

"With your phone?"

"I'm going to explain."

"I found the bookstore you were talking about. Just like you described it, there was not a bigger one in that area. The bookstore display window also contained hardcover books."

"Right, that's what I remember."

"When I went to the bookstore, I went directly to the middle shelf as you described. I faced the window. I put my hand in the middle of the shelf, picked a book and got it. Meanwhile, the seller approached me. He asked if there was a specific book I was looking for. I said that a friend of mine had seen and examined a book on this shelf before, but she hadn't bought it and now she asked me to buy it for her."

"And then?"

"'What was it about?' he asked, and I said, 'I don't know, but there were quotations in it.'"

"And then?"

"He asked what the quotation was. 'Quotations regarding life guidance,' I said. He said he had no idea. He said they had moved the shelves a few weeks ago. 'Your friend must have looked at the religious books,' he said."

"That's very interesting of me to look at a religious book, I had never noticed it."

"I then asked on what shelves the religious books were. Bu at that moment, I happened to get the book I am holding now. I bought it. I also went to the section of the religious books. There I bought this book with quotations in it. But after buying it, I went through all pages like crazy, but I couldn't find a guiding sentence at first sight."

"Let's see what initially strikes me in this book."

"Have a look at it, then."

"I'm looking... opening a page in the middle. Look what it writes: 'Whoever breaks one's heart and makes that person cry, beware of that person's curse. Because whatever the person wishes before the tears fall to the ground becomes real.'"

"Good sentence."

"I'm picking a page from this book as well."

"Go on, pick one."

"Look what it says, 'Iago's basic need is to constantly place the object (Othello) in a humiliating position characterized by ignorance. In this way, he makes him live the situation he has experienced.'"

"That's interesting too, so it says he got him to live the same thing?"

"Yes, it says so."

"Were these any good to you?"

"I need to think."

"The two sentences sounded the opposite of each other."

"Everything has two handles.

Decide which one to hold. "

Epictetus

"I felt the same way, too."

Olga got up to get another cup of coffee. "I'll bring one for you," she said. But Galina didn't hear, she was immersed in thoughts. When she brought the coffee, she wanted to ask Galina what she had in mind. "Sometimes we exaggerate small things, and sometimes we underestimate big things." "I wonder if you could tell me about it, instead of looking for sentences in books, should we put our heads together and look for a solution? It's not your first problem, and we've solved the previous ones, if you can remember."

"Reading is someone's thinking with someone else's head instead of their own."

Arthur Schopenhauer

"You're right, we've solved them, but this is not the kind of thing I can tell. It is very different this time. I feel defeated…"

"Hmm… You will definitely do the right thing."

"In fact, this is a battle, a challenge…"

"Keep your fighting spirit alive. You might be the one who lost now, but it doesn't matter. My father always says what matters is to be able to stay in the game. Continue to fight back and you can rest assured that you will definitely win!"

Olga thought that Galina was looking for a way out, such as quotations from books to relax herself by making an obsession of everything small or big because her psychology was rather disrupted. She couldn't help doubting if her line of thinking was correct.

"The point of philosophy is to start with something so simple as not to seem worth stating, and to end with something so paradoxical that no one will believe it."

Bertrand Russell

Olga asked, "By the way, how's your relationship going with your boyfriend at work?" Galina replied, "Routine, just work, nothing but bed out of work." After a little pause, "So doesn't he spare time for you, or he doesn't have time?" asked Olga. "Both actually," Galina replied.

"Never waste yourself on someone who doesn't have time for you."

Charles Bukowski

"If you are important to someone, s/he creates opportunities for you in any case."

Charles Bukowski

"I hope you will be with someone who appreciates you."

"It's hard to find someone out of work with so much to do."

(Laughing) "I think you can find him. Don't be so hardheaded."

"I think you have someone in mind."

"Yes."

"I don't want anyone in my life right now, believe me."

"Let's eat together, we'll get a little relief."

"Who is it then?"

"His name is Denis Zaytsev. He is someone I used to know, but we are not close. He got divorced from his wife a few years back. I follow him on social media. Previously, he was the mayor."

"Hmm... We could actually meet..."

"Let me see a photo of him on the internet, will you? "

"Hold on, I'll find one."

"..."

"Here you go!"

"Oh, he's handsome, but I'll pass because he has elections again soon."

A Week Later

Galina had gradually started to accept what Doruk had done to her. She was feeling desperate. What else could she do except for resigning herself to reality? She could not continue to get herself used. She ultimately went beyond the stages of falling in love and disappointment and started to confront the reality. Just like many relationships, Galina's relationship had followed the same path.

She didn't know what to do and could not decide on anything either. Instead of waiting for a miracle, she should use her head to get her life together. There was no point in waiting for someone to come and save her.

"No one who believes in truth can witness a miracle."

Kafka

"If one day you feel desperate, don't expect a savior, be the savior yourself."

Mustafa Kemal Atatürk

She would not let herself be the putty in Doruk's plans and Grigory's hands. She had to find someone to get her out of the service, someone with whom she could have children and put her life back on track. She decided to talk to Olga to meet Denis.

She had to find a direction for her life. Having experienced bad things in the past should not prevent her from living good things in the future. It was always possible to enter heaven. She could have a child and raise her child in a family environment.

> *"Heaven has not disappeared because we are all expelled from heaven."*
>
> **Kafka**
>
> *"A happy family is an early heaven."*
>
> **George Bernard Shaw**

Before realizing her thoughts, she would talk to Grigory and tell him that she now wanted to get married and have children, and in a way, she would ask for permission. But before she did that, she muttered to herself, "Let's meet this guy first."

When Galina told Grigory that the source in Turkey wanted a meet, Grigory just told her to take care of herself though he knew that she would be with the source. This showed that Grigory had never accepted her into his life. Galina had paid the price of her betrayal by risking her life for the service and saving her country's dignity.

Galina did not think it was necessary to discuss this with Grigory, even in person. When she entered his room with a small piece of paper, she would say, "I'd like you to read this paper."

Grigory didn't show any reaction when he took the paper and read it.

Galina asked, "You got nothing to say?" Grigory slowly lifted his neck, raising his eyes from the paper towards Galina, and just said, "What you wish is normal, I do understand you."

They had never talked about their relationship and their thoughts about each other. Although they had not been together for a long time, they felt like they had been together for ages due to their work history. The "no-talk agreement" on their relationship was now broken. Galina had been intending to break it for a long time.

When she left Grigory's room, she was both happy and pissed off. Although it was only a part of the plan, she had lived with him and had saved his entire career by risking her life.

She headed back to Grigory's room and walked in without knocking. "Well, does the poison and antidote prevent me from having children, or delay it in some way?" she asked. "The poison only damages the respiratory system. It was meant to kill. No side effects," he replied. Galina liked Grigory's straightforwardness and unhesitant eye contact. He did not start the sentence with such persuasive expressions as "I assure you," "as it is described in the instructions for the poison and antidote and so on," or "I was expecting you to ask me this question," which pointed to the validity of the response she got.

"The naked truth is always the most beautiful, and the simpler its expression, the deeper the impression it will leave."

Arthur Schopenhauer

*

When she got home, her mother asked, "Gala, you are okay, aren't you?"

"Yes, mom."

"Be careful with what you eat the next time. See? Every day they talk about the new bacteria on TV."

"You're right, mom. But we usually eat out, and we try to choose decent places."

Galina had asked Inga to call her mother and tell her that she had food poisoning, and that the service was at the hospital so that her mother would not worry. Her mother had wanted to come to the hospital, but only the service staff was allowed at the hospital for the treatment or visit. Her mother was very nervous and repeatedly asked Inga if there was anything else. Inga had visited her mother twice to give her assurance.

Having done these things for the job, Inga was getting closer to Galina. Galina thought that she was fine with this rapprochement, but something was bothering her at the same time. She did not want to give Inga an upper hand.

CHAPTER 3

PRODUCT OF HATE

11 Months Later

Courtroom

Denis was dizzy and having a blackout because of the talks. He sighed, "If I had been jailed pending trial, I couldn't have stood that, and I could have died." He was only banned from travelling abroad. Denis felt like screaming very loud. He was feeling as if he were drowning in the courtroom.

A male judge, who was in his fifties and wearing glasses, raised his head from the file and looked towards Denis and his attorney.

Denis's attorney Yegor stood up and began to speak. While Yegor was talking, Denis felt as if he were unable to hear what he was saying. He was merely thinking, "What if I am not acquitted..." He focused on Yegor's speech on the spur of the moment. It was as if he suddenly started to hear. Yegor: "As you can see, no criterion that is acceptable to the High Court of Appeals[2] has been materialized in this case. The case is based entirely on fiction. I would like to inform you here on behalf of my client that we will not bring any complaints against the plaintiff Ms. Irina provided that she admits to slandering my client and that I am ready to be her legal representative if need be."

The judge, examining the report through the gap over his glasses, looked at Irina and her lawyer and said,

"Yes, I'm listening."

Irina touched her lawyer's arm as if expressing her desire to speak and stood up.

"Your Honor, I am a single woman who lives alone. My father died when I was very young. My mother also died when I started middle school. I clung to life and have sailed through the challenges of life. That's why I wanted my child to grow up with a mother," she said and began to cry.

"Go on."

---

[2] Supreme Court of Russia

"I can't stand this any longer. Please save me. Some people threatened to kill me if I did not slander Denis, and they would kill me, and my child would grow up in orphanages just like me."

"So, you admit that there really isn't such a thing, right?"

"Yes, and they said, 'We had him dismissed before, he couldn't do anything, and he can't do anything to you, either.'"

Everyone's eyes, including the judge, were wide open. The court room was stunned into silence.

"So, you accept that it is a slander?"

"Yes, but I had to do it to save my child."

"Look, if they threatened you to testify this way, say it here because it will not be easy for you to turn back from this confession."

"I'm telling the truth."

"And who were the people that threatened you?"

"I don't know them."

"When did it happen?"

"A few weeks after I started living with Denis, I saw a black car several times on our way with my child to my friends.

"What make was the car?"

"I don't remember the brand, but it was an ordinary car. It wasn't the kind of car that would attract much attention."

"How did it attract your attention then?"

"While I was putting my child in the back seat, this particular black car slowed down and lowered its black window."

"What kind of a person was inside?"

"The driver had a shaved head, was wearing thin glasses that were hardly noticeable on his face."

"What did you think when you saw him?"

"I thought he confused me with someone and ignored him."

"A few days passed by. Denis wasn't home and I left the house to take my child to see a doctor. While I was leaving the doctor's office, that man approached me again. He said, 'If you don't slander Denis saying that you caught him rubbing his genitals against your child, your child will grow up just like you, on his own.'"

"What did you say?"

"I froze and I initially thought he was sort of joking at first."

"'Do you understand what I'm saying?' said the man."

"The judge turned towards the side of the defendant and let Denis's lawyer speak."

"It has been understood by the sincere confession of the plaintiff that the incident was a slander. I demand the acquittal of my client."

Denis was looking at the judge's face. His knees were shaking. The judge stood up and so did the rest of the hall. He spruced up his black robe, got the book with a red cover and the inscription of 'On Behalf of the Russian Federation' on it, and carrying a twin-headed eagle symbolizing the Russian Federation he announced,

"Acquitted!"

When they came out of the courtroom, they were overwhelmed by journalists. Denis and his lawyer were speaking to the media's microphones to make their statements.

Yegor said, "As a result of the power of our defense and the truth, the plaintiff admitted to slandering my client. Tomorrow we will present our petition to the attorney general, Ministry of Internal Affairs and the Kremlin to start an investigation in order to reveal the connection between this slander and previous dismissal of my client from his duty as the mayor."

When they arrived at Yegor's office, the news had already been on the internet.

The acquittal was reported as breaking news. Their favorite headlines were that of Pravda and Vesti; "Got Him Dismissed But Not Jailed," "Dismissal Was a Conspiracy."

11 Months Earlier

Olga called Denis and said, "Denis, long time no see! Let's meet and talk about the time we haven't seen each other and your rise in your career." Denis responded, "Well, my career is on decline, but I will meet you for sure," and they set the meet-up. Olga always introduced Galina as her "cousin" for they were very close, and she informed Denis that her cousin might accompany her.

Before the meet-up, Galina left work and stopped by her home. She changed her clothes, refreshed her makeup and put on her favorite perfume.

She looked into the mirror and said, "Yes, I look terrific in this jacket." It was her favorite dark blue jacket.

Galina called Olga and asked, "Hello Ol, where are you?" "We are just sitting, what about you?" said Olga. Galina replied, "On my way to my love!"

"One of the cages has gone looking for a bird."

Kafka

When Galina arrived, Olga and Denis were absorbed in intimate talk. With a smile on her face, Galina interrupted the conversation saying, "If I am interrupting, I can come later."

Olga introduced them, "Oh, no... Galina, Denis." Rising to his feet, Denis said, "Welcome and nice to meet you."

From the heavy conversation she understood that Denis wanted to be elected mayor again and was looking for a way out in the Duma[3] elections afterwards. Galina said, "Denis, I think we need to draw a roadmap for you to get to the summit again." Denis asked, "Can you do this?" Olga intervened, "Do not underestimate Galina. She is not an interpreter actually."

"What do you do?"

"I'm a police officer."

"Superb. Can you find out who is messing with me?"

"I'll have a look into it."

"Not just looking! It needs a serious investigation."

"I'll investigate it."

"I can't tell you how important this is to me."

---

[3] The lower Wing of the Russian Parliament

"You know so many people. Why couldn't you get it investigated?"

"Because when the people to be investigated are high-level and there is some investigation about them, your system reports to Kremlin and they want to know why there is an investigation."

"Yes, in such cases a special authorization might be needed. But our unit is a bit different. I can check it. Getting permission from my director would be enough."

"What if he doesn't give the permission?"

"I don't think he will turn me down."

"I'm ready to do whatever is necessary for this."

"There is no need for what you are trying to say."

"All right, but still I want you know that I'm ready."

"Look, here we are in a friendly environment, so stop this politics. If I need something, I will tell you right away. If you can send me the cell phone numbers of the people you suspect, I can start looking into them."

"Sure, can you really find these people?"

"I will, but on one condition."

"Which is?"

"Will you take me out for a dinner if I find?"

Olga bursts into laughter.

"Sure."

"If I can't, I will take you."

"Agreed."

"But in the meantime, there is something I want you to do."

"Of course. What is it?"

"You need to relax a little. While you are narrating the events, it is like you are still experiencing them like the very first day. I believe you can benefit from a psychologist's advice. I also get help at difficult times and so far, it has proven to be very helpful."

"All right, I'll have an appointment as soon as possible."

"If you visit the psychologist before our next meeting, you will get the chance to evaluate better what I am going to tell you."

"All right, deal."

"By the way, why didn't you get married again after divorce?"

"You need to have a plan of life for marriage."

"Why don't you have one?"

"Whenever I make a plan and put things in an order, something unexpected occurs."

"Is it always the same?"

"In significant times and on significant matters."

"Hmm."

"I can decide to marry only after I sign the book and have the photos taken. Nothing I want has been realized in full, anyway."

*

When Galina came home, she thought about how powerful Denis was and whether he was rich. "If he didn't have the power, he wouldn't have been the mayor. He has lost some altitude, but his core needs to be unearthed and he needs to stand up," she murmured.

God gives the nuts, but he does not crack them."

Kafka

She was suddenly startled by a message from Doruk and got lost in thoughts. Doruk was asking to meet with her again. With the never-ending hate and the desire of revenge in her, she got the phone. Her mind had been continuously busy with what she would do to him and how to take revenge on him. Her love was as big as her hatred. She loved him as much as she hated him.

She spent some time on a few web pages on the phone and texted Doruk, "I missed you too. How about a short three-day vacation in Spain on the sixth of next month?"

"That would be great!" Doruk replied.

The next morning Galina woke up early to check the list Denis had given to her. She established the chain of telephone contacts in the system after doing some research over the internet.

The sequence of phone conversations between certain contacts before and after certain events put everything in broad daylight.

The animosity went as far as to a person whose face Denis had never seen before. The man in question was the previous deputy mayor and he had ignited the events. Before Denis was elected mayor or even announced his candidacy, in order not to lose his seat, he had made a so-called press announcement that he had been asked his opinion regarding a pro-USA and EU revolution similar to the Orange Revolution and that he had been offered a political bribe to support the revolution. To promote his claim, he had not neglected to file a complaint at the prosecutor's office.

Since the Russians came from a secret service tradition in which the agents pretended to defect to the USA and thus misled the CIA, they were cautious about such methods and they would investigate whether the activity was authentic and what the real motive was behind it. In her research, Galina analyzed that this man was in fact a supporter of the USA and the EU, and that in order to guarantee his seat and to create diversion from his destructive activities he needed such a fictitious story. He had already not been nominated by his party due to his corrupted activities and relations with the USA and the EU behind the scenes, and as his relations would cause damage to his party, this issue had been silently covered up.

This sly former deputy mayor continued his destructive activities even when he was not in the office and he was busy producing disinformation about Denis. He was going from door to door to spread such slanders as "The mayor is supporting the Sorosian revolution," addressing the hardcore anti-revolutionists. This group took the matter to the previous Duma president who also spread the rumor to the current Duma president. The mayor was relieved of duty by Kremlin without any further investigation.

All of these details showed that the events were a lot more far-reaching and multidimensional than Denis had imagined.

*

Denis made an appointment with his psychologist. The psychologist was surprised to receive a call from Denis after so many years. She was curious about what had happened in Denis's life. She checked his file again and added his appointment after the last appointment of the next day.

When Denis went to Ms. Marina's office, he noticed that the secretary at the office had changed. The secretary called Ms. Marina and informed her that Denis was there. Meanwhile, Denis was taking sips from the water he had asked while he was waiting. "Even after many years, the counselee and the counselor cannot break the connection, and it is inevitable for the secretary to intervene," Denis muttered.

Denis went upstairs following a call from Ms. Marina to her secretary. Just as he was about to knock on the door, Ms. Marina stepped out of the adjacent bathroom.

"Welcome Denis," gesturing at him to go into the room with her hand.

"Thank you, Ms. Marina."

"How are you?"

"I'm fine, and you?"

"I'm fine too, thanks a lot."

"It's been a long time, right?"

"Well, let me think, it's been 5 years now I believe."

"My notes say it's been 6 years."

"That's true, time flies."

"Yes, but I see you're doing well."

"Not actually."

"Tell me, I'm listening."

Denis briefly described the events he had been through.

"I'm glad you have solved your problems with women. I had written in my notes that your IQ was high."

"Thanks."

"I'm not using this as a placebo."

"…"

"Are you using the medicine you've just mentioned regularly?"

"Yes."

"First of all Denis, you know when you are sitting in a political chair, everything can happen to you in that chair. You must have an idea of what might happen because you're a smart person."

"Right."

"You took the risk and still wanted to sit in that chair. 'When in battle, one is likely to get wounded,' you know that. Everything seldomly goes well."

"Yes."

"Now, first and foremost, you should know this. You're not supposed to take it personally. It's of course a difficult situation, but it's clear that you're not the target but rather it is the state apparatus and the Kremlin that represent your political ideas."

"Yes."

"Therefore, it is clear that the events triggered by your refusal to do projects with EU budgets are actually an attempt against the state, not against you."

"Right."

"You have to understand this very well and never forget this fact."

"So, are you still being targeted?"

"Yes, I am. The people that are connected to the people who are operating against me are trying to understand whether I will make a counter-attack or if I have found the perpetrators of the events."

"Apart from this?"

"They're trying to get me into trouble, but they don't have any evidence."

"So, do you have any idea why they're still messing with you?"

"Yes, I do. Because during my duty, I refused to accept EU funding and set an example for all municipalities. They could not take this blow."

"Let me ask the question in this way, is there anything in your hand that might be a threat to them?"

"No, because I gave them all to the relevant units."

"I don't think they have any motive to mess with you. I hope the relevant units didn't push things under the rug."

"I don't think so."

"Still, whatever document and information you have, send it to several government agencies through different channels so that they will hear that you have shared everything with the state and understand that you have nothing else against them. This is really important."

"You are right."

"Denis, you see, when you are a psychologist in Moscow, these things become part of your job. Because what matters is that we make you feel comfortable. The events that have happened to you require more than psychological counseling..."

"I noticed that. I think you have many clients like me."

"There are a few."

"Great."

"You shouldn't plan your life anymore and lose your spontaneity."

"So?"

"Let me put it this way, there is curiosity, excitement, joy and compassion in the moment. You should live the moment and not adopt any idea outside the moment. These feelings are only in the moment. To stay in the moment, you need to keep your mind vigorous and do sports regularly. For example, famous writers say that 'inspiration comes when walking.'"

"Yes."

"The body becomes activated when it warms up and connects with the mind. To be fluent, to be vigilant and most importantly to be in the moment, sports is a must."

"Right."

"You can't be spontaneous when you're worried. You get worried when you think about the past. Moreover, the founder of Psychodrama, describes spontaneity as 'here and now.' So, you should be here and now."

"I will try."

"So, are you trying to get back to the same place?"

"Yes."

"So, do you really want to? Or ..."

"I really want to."

"Now would you stand up and come to my desk?"

"Sure."

"Now close your eyes and think of a white wall in front of you. Look at all the four corners of this wall."

"..."

"Did you look?"

"Yes."

"Try to see the width of the wall at one glance and thoroughly examine the surface of the wall, let yourself go, relax..."

"..."

"Okay, now, if your answer to a question is yes, stretch forward or right, if no, stretch back or left."

"Do you really want to go back to the duty?"

Denis stretched forward.

"Do you want to return to the duty for yourself?"

Denis stretched forward.

"Yes, you can open your eyes."

"..." Denis returned to his seat.

"Well, what has changed in your life after these events?"

"I'm not leaving the house without a gun."

"What else?"

"I'm constantly trying to be cautious, thinking that this pro-West group might conspire against me and have me locked up."

"Do you fear death?"

"Yes."

"What comes to your mind is from your unconscious, so it's you, always telling you to be careful. When you hear these whispers, try saying 'Thanks, I'm being careful.'"

"Got it."

"Your mind, that is your ego, wants to get appreciated, and your unconscious doesn't."

"Hmm…"

"You started this job to build a career, but now you've brought it to the point of 'all or nothing', that is, 'I will die for this job', right?"

"Yes. What exactly was the previous test?"

"With this test, we try to learn the person's real thoughts by getting support from the body when the person's mind is very active or constantly working. Because during such periods, we may not be able to get the real answer from the mind and it can mislead us. In a sense, the body communicates with the mind and gives us the right answer. The reality is always what the body feels. Leaning to the left was no, and to the back was fear."

"An interesting method!"

"Now that you have turned the idea of returning to this duty again into an ideal; this way of thinking does not belong to you. You have exaggerated the success there and the pleasure you felt when you turned down the western block has become an obsession for you; returning to the duty or trying to do so might bring your end... you must quickly get rid of this idea of reaching a target..."

*

Denis was impatient.

When they met, Galina looked into Denis's eyes like a naughty girl.

She was not surprised that Denis asked without even saying hello, "Did you find anything?"

Galina replied, "Yes, I figured it out."

After a long conversation, Galina said, "I also have a plan to get you out of this bottleneck."

"Very nice, what is it?"

"Getting this man to talk, proving that he slandered you, or..."

"No way, he won't talk. "Or what?"

"Or making him slander you again and connecting both slanders to vindicate your reputation."

"Genius! Are you a policewoman or a politician?"

"I'm not a cop actually. I work for intelligence."

"Is that where your skill in fiction comes from?"

"Probably."

After this conversation, Denis suddenly quit his stiff stance and began to relax, sitting comfortably in his chair. He ordered another bottle of wine. Galina wasn't drinking. For the first time, she was not responding to a man's flirting in an alcoholic environment. Galina would no longer be anyone's toy.

"No one can look down on you unless you allow it."

Eleanor Roosevelt

But somehow, she wanted to get pregnant. In doing so, she had no intention of conceding herself. She would play the game by her rules.

Never compromise yourself. You are all you've got."

Janis L. Joplin

So, she got closer to Denis and said, "Don't worry, everything's going to be all right. Wars are won by strategy, not by sadness," and began kissing Denis. Denis could not even respond to Galina's kisses because of his demoralization and the influence of alcohol. "What if he uses contraception while making love to me?" she thought suddenly. Then she thought, "I'll take his sperm off the ground and pour it into my body, and I'll even take it out of the trash if necessary."

Denis was heavily drunk by the time they arrived at his house. He didn't even take off his shoes. He went straight up to the stairs and slowly tried to climb them, only to fail in his efforts. He grabbed the railing. Galina supported him from behind. Denis headed for the bed. Galina checked the bedroom from the corner of her eye. There were no signs of a female's presence. Denis was already buried in bed.

Galina took her clothes off. Denis's eyes were closed. "I promise I will make a hero out of you," she said. Denis barely opened his eyes, staring at Galina, "Really?" he asked. Galina said, "Yes." Then she touched Denis's genitals…

When Galina got out of the bed in the morning, out of habit, she immediately checked the bee pollen pills she used to take to get pregnant from Doruk. The reason she hadn't drunk alcohol last night was the idea that the pills could lose their effect. There were a few more in the box. She used these pills all the time to support her ovaries. In fact, there wasn't a problem with her ovaries. Doruk's fictions had caused Galina to feel unhealthy.

*

She was extremely happy when she got to the Center. The gratitude in the eyes of Denis when he woke up was vividly before her eyes. This caused Galina to think that Denis would be in her life from then on and his presence would give her strength. Another reason that made Galina feel good was that she saw how easy it was to handle people when they were drunk when she was not under the influence of alcohol herself. She had never thought she could take advantage of a drunk man. "It looks as if the sides and roles are now changing," she thought.

> *"You have to learn the rules of the game and then to play better than anyone…"*
>
> **Albert Einstein**

But what really made her happy was the feeling and possibility of being pregnant. Walking down the corridor, she felt like she had wings.

When she arrived at her desk, she quickly opened the Chinese calendar on the internet. "Yesterday was a good day," she murmured. A good day to get pregnant.

She started to search about pregnancy and its signs on the internet. The topic of hysterical pregnancy was almost on all web pages. Hysterical pregnancy was a false pregnancy in which nausea, weight gain, sensitivity in the breasts, lactation and even the growth of the abdomen could be observed. As a result of hormonal changes, even pregnancy tests could give false-positive results, and the mother could even feel the baby's kick. For this reason, it was recommended that the woman should be checked multiple times by a doctor. Extreme desire to get pregnant, seeking self-confidence, self-esteem, a sense of identity, a strong urge to get rid of loneliness, seeking attention from the husband, family and environment and the mind's attempt to defeat the feeling of biological failure could cause hysterical pregnancy. The condition was reported to be more common in women who never got pregnant.

In addition to pregnancy which she wanted for her spiritual ascent, she also needed power and money for her material self. It would not be possible to leave the SVR without a powerful reference or plenty of money. Otherwise she would have to attempt suicide several times, which was too risky. This could go beyond attempt and she could die.

She could solve power and money issues by clearing Denis or using different people other than Denis. But Denis was easy-to-reach and she could add power to money. So, she had to vindicate Denis and make him popular.

Besides all this, Galina had so many question marks in her head. She was getting older; would she be able to get pregnant? Was it ever possible that Doruk really loved her? Could she leave the service? Were the Americans after her? Was it a coincidence that Inga built a close relationship with her, or was it due to the course of events? Or because they suspected that she was spying for the Turks? Had the Fetullah Terrorist Organization (FETÖ), which they called "gravediggers", delivered Doruk's real identity and the lists and photographs to other services besides the Greek Intelligence? Would these lists reach the SVR indirectly? Could the lists be sold by auction?

As the unconscious did not perceive the past or the future and obey the orders given to it, Galina began to give herself positive commands. For this reason, instead of fearsome expressions, she created affirmative statements that would comfort her: "I will get pregnant and raise my child because I have the right to do so," "I will pull my life together because I deserve it," "I will not be compromised and I will not compromise people around me because I'm right."

When she went home in the evening, she took her mother's cell phone. She would record these sentences in a sincere, genuine and serene tone. At night she would clean the unconscious while lying, that is, when the alpha frequency was on and the unconscious was open. But she could not record the same sentences on her mother's phone. If the SVR operated on her, the voice recordings could be captured. That's why, she prepared suitable affirmative statements by doing research on YouTube. "I will succeed," "I will be happy," "Life is easy for me," "I want to live," "Money and power are with me," and "I will set myself free from all problems." After preparing the sentences, she wrote "at least 21 days of affirmative statements" in the notes section of the phone. She knew that this method might not work if she listened less than twenty-one days.

"... Fear may come true that which one is afraid of... "

Viktor E. Frankl

*

She had to learn more about Doruk and the ideology he belonged to. But she could not get new results by repeatedly examining Doruk's file. In an inconspicuous way, she decided to conduct a research from open sources in order to find out about the state ideal of the Turks whom Doruk belonged to. When she came to the Center's library, she enjoyed the silence, there was not a single sound. As she moved towards the computers where the library archive was registered, the sound of her steps echoed in the hall. She pulled a chair and sat down at the table. She searched the words "Turkish Union" on the library computer. She glanced at many sources that appeared on the screen. She wrote the number of the article on a book request slip, stood up, smoothed down her skirt and walked towards the staff desk.

"I don't need to write down the name of the article, I guess, as there is this number."

"Let me check it. Just a sec."

"..."

"Is the article called 'The Road to Turan?'"

After the staff printed the article, Galina signed the form containing the name of the article, the section, language and number of pages, and the information about the place where it was published. While Galina was signing the form, she planned her answer to a possible question such as "Why did you read this article?" She decided to say, "It was one of the current issues I saw on television and so that my Turkish would not get rusty."

She moved towards the table and read the article without a pause. The article stated that the Turkish Union's objective was to unite the Turks living in the independent states of Turkey, Azerbaijan, Kazakhstan, Kyrgyzstan, Uzbekistan, Turkmenistan, and Northern Cyprus with the Turks living without an independent country in other countries like Iraq and Iran, the Uyghur Turks, those living in the states of Altai, Bashkortostan, Gagauz, Khakassia, Yakut and Tatarstan under the flag of a country called Turan. First of all, it was necessary to fulfill the abolition of customs and visas and the establishment of a common army among the countries in question. In addition, the British Colonies' uniting to form the United States, and the Arabs' uniting and establishing the Arab League were mentioned as examples. However, it was stated that without serving the American Imperialism and the division and civil war in the above-mentioned countries, autonomous structures should be strengthened gradually in the historical process of the establishment of the Turan state.

The article continued with the examples from the European Union. It was emphasized that even the conflicting societies could unite. The views of deputies living outside Turkey such as Ganira Pashayeva, who was a deputy in the parliament when this article was written and who believed in this ideal state, were also widely discussed in the article. At the same time, the article included the views of deputy Vladimir Zhirinovsky, who previously presided over the Russian Parliament's lower house, Duma, and is currently the Liberal Democratic Party's Chairman, claiming that Turkey's army had become the most powerful army of NATO, that the population of Turkic countries would reach 500 million in a short time, that their language would pave the way for a union and that they would ultimately establish "the Great Turkish Republic of Turan."

Towards the end of the article, there were some historical details such as the efforts to establish the Idil-Ural State in the region where Tatars and Bashkirs lived within the Soviet borders, and the Muslim command within the Red Army. It was also mentioned that thinkers like Sultan Galiyev believed in Turanism during the Soviet Union period. Galina was baffled by what she had just read. When she read in the footnote of the article about Stalin's order to get Galiyev killed, including the murders of his wife and daughter after being raped, she got very emotional and felt sad.

For a moment, Galina thought, "Was it my Tatar blood that caused me to fall in love with Doruk?" When she raised her head and looked at the clock, she decided to download one more article before leaving to meet Grigory.

She sat at a computer table to search for an article. She typed the words "Turkey and democracy" in current articles section and picked the one titled "The Development of Democracy in Turkey."

It was so boring. Still, since she respected the tree that was used for the paper, she continued and finished the whole article.

Then, she gave both articles to the person in charge and asked them to be shredded. The staff printed a form for the shredding of the articles and made Galina sign it.

While she was waiting for the lift, she thought about a piece of information she learned from the article. Ataturk had granted Turkish women's suffrage very early in comparison to many western countries and she reflected on the developments that occurred as a result of women's protection of the ballots in Aslankoy district of Mersin. Then she muttered, "These Turks are really interesting people," and confessed to herself that she was impressed by the women's movement.

A Week Later

When she woke up that morning, Galina was feeling something different about herself. She got out of the bed, put her slippers on and looked into the mirror. All of a sudden, she had an epiphany. She put on her clothes and rushed out into the street. Her mom was startled by the banging of the door. When Galina returned home, her mother, Dasha, asked her, "Where did you go this early in the morning? I called you and you didn't pick up." Galina replied, "I had to go out to get something, nothing important," and headed for the bathroom. The test result was positive. She couldn't believe her eyes. She almost hugged the test kit. She spent a few minutes looking at herself in the mirror, not knowing what to do.

Then, she jumped out again and went back to the pharmacy. She asked the girl at the pharmacy, "Hi again, is the test I just bought reliable?" The girl replied, "I gave you the best quality kit. The results are always 95-99 percent true." She was in seventh heaven leaving the pharmacy. This was the happiest moment of her life. She started dreaming about raising her child and the beautiful clothes she would buy for her baby.

Thoughts chased one another in her mind. "Perhaps what I really needed was not Doruk but a child," she thought for a moment and "If I am really pregnant, now is the time to figure out the matter with Doruk." She decided not to share the news with anyone until her pregnancy was certain. Doruk was still in her mind. "Maybe if it weren't for Doruk, I wouldn't be so sure about getting pregnant and having a child..."

Had all the suffering been a step towards the fulfillment of her goals, reorganizing her life and reaching happiness?

The way to reach happiness and be satisfied
with life is not avoiding suffering but seeing it as a
natural step that we will definitely come across
while trying to attain what is good."

Nietzsche

"If you call what you come across an
obstacle, you trip and fall down; if you call it a
step, you go one step up."

La Edri

All these thoughts were still not enough to forgive Doruk. She was unable to pull herself together to forgive him, for she had judged herself so harshly when she saw Doruk unmasked.

"You never use those excuses for yourself which you
find in order to forgive others."

Dagville

Doruk would not want things to happen this way either! But here was the outcome. The causes did not matter!

"There is no need to know the unique intentions of an
artist. The work will explain everything."

Susan Sontag

She murmured, "Betrayal does not have a cause but a price," as Turks often expressed. At the end of the day, Doruk had betrayed her. That was the result. And it wouldn't change because it was real.

Each service would fight relentlessly against threats to the interests of the country and the happiness and security of its people. Galina and Doruk were at war, too. Entering a war meant getting wounded. That was natural. She should have known this. She should have looked for the faults in herself, not in Doruk. Galina thought that there was a war-free zone in the war, and she was totally wrong. The sirens of war had been heard from the first day she joined the service. This siren would continue to sound until after she left the service, and even later.

"People who can't hear the music think dancers are crazy."

Nietzsche

"There is no middle way in wartime."

Winston Churchill

Suddenly, she thought, "Maybe everything would have happened differently if she and Doruk had fought on the same side." She did not want the service, the war and the cruel rules of war in her life after her baby was born.

She discarded her positive thoughts about Doruk. He would remain to be the enemy. She said, "fuso"[4] to herself. Doruk's positive influence on Galina did not eliminate the enmity in her but merely turned him into a respected enemy.

"You may have enemies whom you hate, but not enemies whom you despise. You must be proud of your enemy."

Nietzsche

Her enmity to Doruk gave her courage and audacity.

"The real enemy gives you unlimited courage."

Kafka

When she came home, she closed her door, leaned against it and burst into tears. Her mother walked curiously towards Galina's room.

"Gala, what's going on? You keep going out and coming back."

"Everything is all right, no problem."

"Gala, would you please open the door? You don't sound well. Come on, open it!"

Galina wiped her tears and opened the door.

"What happened?"

"Mom, I got some good news, but let me not share it even with you for the time being. Give me a couple of weeks."

---

[4] That's enough

"Fine."

"…"

For a moment they looked at each other in silence.

"Are you pregnant?"

"I think I am."

Galina said the sentence "I'm pregnant" so naively, but she thought everything could break apart in a moment. She seemed to think of this experience as a sweet dream and was trying to hide her joy even from herself. She was so scared. She couldn't believe the test result was positive and was very surprised that she got pregnant so easily.

Suddenly, two questions flocked her mind: Had the treatment worked? And had Doruk used a contraceptive method to prevent her from getting pregnant? It didn't matter anymore. Because she was feeling her pregnancy now.

"Everything has a time.

Neither does the rose blossom before its time,

Nor does the sun rise earlier.

Wait, what is yours will come to you."

Rumi

"Something that seems distant and impossible may be close and possible in an instant."

Tolstoy

Was Denis going to change his life? Was it a coincidence that she got pregnant at their first sexual intercourse?

"There is no such thing as coincidence: God doesn't play dice."

Albert Einstein

A few days had passed, and she was trying to get used to her new emotional state. She was so confused. She had to make a plan about Doruk and reorganize her life. All of a sudden, she decided to go out to Gorki Park and do some brisk walking rather than staying home on Sunday. She called Olga to invite her, but Olga said she was not in the mood.

Galina arrived at Gorki Park and started to walk briskly. Everything seemed so beautiful and she looked at the children in the park thinking, "What will my child look like?" Keeping in mind Denis's facial and physical features, she amused herself saying, "Maybe my baby will look like the child running with some food in his hands."

Her mind got clearer as she walked. She had to plan thoroughly to achieve happiness. She muttered, "I must take my revenge on Doruk," and increased her speed. She didn't want to forgive him. She would never let anyone play with her. Optimism was not part of her life anymore.

> *"There comes a time when there is no return from a road, no excuse for some mistakes, no meaning of some people."*
>
> ### Ivan Turgenyev

She decided to kill Doruk. She could not do this with her own gun, so she needed an unlicensed one. Finding an unlicensed gun in Moscow was an easy task. But it would cause her trouble if she found it herself. The center would put her under investigation if it came out.

She thought of what she had to do. She could find one if she went to a night club where drugs are dealt. Then she thought of Denis. Their interests were common now. When she saw Denis,

"Denis, do you know anyone who can get us an unlicensed gun?"

"For what?" he said being totally surprised.

"For every household must have an unlicensed gun."

"Let me look into it, then."

"All right, but it should be unused and not Russian made."

A few days later, Denis called Galina and told her to come to his house. Galina figured that Denis wanted to show the guns in his house. She quickly went there wearing the wig she had previously used for Grigory. Then she took the taxi waiting at her front door and went to see Denis.

When Denis opened the door, he was baffled to see Galina with a wig. Galina said, "There is no harm in some disguise." Denis responded, "So, you understood I called you in for the gun. I'm impressed, indeed. But why are you wearing a wig?"

When they got into the living room, the brunette man with grey hair stood up. "This is Agop," said Denis.

"Hi, I'm Katya."

"Nice to meet you."

"Me, too."

"If you tell me exactly what kind of pistol you want, I can bring you all the brands and models you want."

"I'm thinking of 6.35."

"You want a classic lady gun apparently."

"Kind of."

"What about the bullet capacity?"

"At least 5 +1."

"But it is not easy to find unused pistols of these barrel diameters."

"Then, let's look for a model whose barrel we can change."

"Wow, I love people who know about guns."

Galina threw a smile.

"If you could soon find a gun that is clean, all parts black, not coated or a little coated, Baby Browning or an equivalent, that would be great."

"Okay. I'm the most renowned gun dealer in Moscow. I will bring you very good models."

"Great!"

"So, is there a price range?"

"Price doesn't matter as long as the mechanism is solid."

"Got it."

"When do we meet again?"

"I'll be here tomorrow at the same time, if that's okay with you?"

Galina looked at Denis.

"Okay."

"See you tomorrow then."

The next day, when they met again at Denis's home, Agop was staring and smiling at Galina.

"It is evident from your face that you have brought some nice guns."

"Yes. Let me show you right away."

Agop took out the boxes lined up in a small bag. All three boxes were the same. They were brown and encrypted. He opened the boxes. Galina was excited. Denis was looking into Galina's eyes and trying to measure her reaction.

"Yeah, look, this is Baby Browning. Very little used. Coated a few years ago. 5 +1."

"Yes, it looks good. If you can dismantle it, we can see the inner parts."

"Let me show you the others, and maybe you will not want them dismantled."

"Sure."

"Look, this one is a very famous German pistol, Lignose's model produced by the Mauser factory. And it is 10 +1."

"Very nice."

"When you look at this pistol, could you understand its features?"

"No, what is it?"

Taking the pistol in his hand, Agop said,

"Look, this part in front of the trigger is made like a trigger. When you pull this, the pistol is cocked. So, since it is cocked with one hand, you don't need to use your other hand."

"Great!"

"This pistol has different names. One-handed pistol, or urban assassination pistol."

"How's the mechanism?"

"In good condition. If you want, I can get a barrel made."

"Can you get it done exactly the same?"

"Yes, of course."

"Very good. Can you show the other one now?"

"Sure."

Agop was enthusiastic as he was opening the third box. Denis was just watching Galina and Agop, without making any comments. Agop grabbed the gun, and he said, "Look, this has the same working principle."

"Yes, it is cocked with one hand, you mean."

"Yes. It's called Praga, and it's so small and ergonomic, which makes it great. Look, the trigger's hidden. It's also cocked over the barrel. See? The trigger falls down when you pull the top of the barrel," he said and pulled the barrel.

"Yes, that's great, but there's a risk of the finger slipping down the cocking area and apparently it has less capacity."

"Yes, that's why I recommend you the Mauser."

"Yes, Mauser's carving is also very nice. The previous owner had some taste."

"The rumor has it that this gun was first produced in 1921. But it was produced in small numbers. Adolf Hitler used to give this pistol to his trusted officers. They were carrying the pistol between the shirt and the uniform in their arms and used it as a last resort weapon."

"It's quite interesting."

"For example, if one officer lost one of his hands, he could cock and use this pistol, and even commit suicide under the most difficult conditions not to surrender to the enemy."

Galina thought it would be very enjoyable to blow Doruk's brain with this weapon and suddenly said, "Okay. We'll get the Mauser."

She took the pistol's box in her hand and said, "Mr. Agop, how many days will it take for the barrel to be ready?"

"Up to 10 days."

"It's okay, if you can get a few hammers made, you'll deliver them all together. And a few boxes of bullets. But not old bullets!"

"Don't worry, Ms. Katya, I never sell old bullets."

"Okay then."

"Should we make alterations to the noses to enhance the impact of the bullets?"

"That would be nice."

"Okay then."

Galina had Denis pay for the pistols and bullets and gave the impression that she was paid off for her favor to Denis. Nobody in Russia would do any favor for free.

Next weekend, Galina went to Gorky Park for another walk. When she arrived at the park, she once again felt some relief inside. The park was full of couples walking hand in hand, children chasing pigeons, teenagers gathered around guitars. There was a queue of people to get coffee. All were happy.

Galina decided that happiness was the most necessary component of life. As days progressed, signs of pregnancy started to manifest themselves one by one. Her happiness also increased with the alleviation of symptoms. She thought she should often go to the doctor and get checked. Then she shifted her thoughts to Doruk.

Her plan became clearer as she walked. She had already been living with plans since the unveiling of Doruk's mask in Greece. She had sworn in Greece, "I will not die until I make you feel what you made me feel."

"People forget what you said or did, but they never forget how you made them feel."

Maya Angelou

She suddenly decided that it would be very simple for her to kill Doruk by shooting him with a pistol. Doruk shouldn't die so easily. She had to kill him in a unique way. Shooting him with a gun was a very ordinary idea.

67

"Choose patient satisfaction, not hasty pleasures."

Epictetus

She combined different fragments into a plan and tried to finetune it in her mind. As a matter of fact, she ended up having two different plans both of which were as crazy as her love for Doruk. It made sense. Her mind was occupied with Doruk all the time. Her love pushed her to make lunatic plans! She couldn't help asking herself, "Am I crazy?"

"There is always some madness in love, but there is also always some reason in madness."

Nietzsche

"Love is a serious mental illness."

Plato

Of course, she needed time, patience and luck to implement her plans and get results.

"The most powerful fighters are time and patience."

Tolstoy

She needed to be strong, believe in her plan and stick to it to get results, and of course luck the foremost.

"There is a driving force more powerful than steam, electricity and atomic energy: the will. "

Albert Einstein

Her plan was ready. Galina was going to commit a perfect murder. But she would not do it with a pistol, rather she would kill Doruk using Iago's tactic, which was written in the book Olga brought from Baku. She would kill him so badly that Doruk would turn into a living dead.

"The most perfect murder is to kill someone's joy of living."

Paulo Coelho

Ankara

When Doruk approached the airport, he saw that the vehicles were inching their way through the heavy traffic.

He was thinking about the dream he had the night before he was assigned the duty about Galina. This dream haunted his mind several times a day despite all the time that had passed. In his dream he was going down a winding slide in an aquapark. As he went down the slide, he saw a woman in white sneakers just before him, clothed in a veil like the black shroud of Azrael. He spread his arms sideways to avoid hitting her. Thus, he managed to stop. But then the water-level of the pool rose and left him breathless. In the meantime, he suddenly started to rise into the sky, taking a deep breath and awakening.

He checked the time. "I hope I'll catch up," he murmured. He couldn't wait to get off the taxi when he saw the domestic departures gate. "Am I in a hurry to get to work or to Galina?" he asked himself.

He was monitoring people's behavior before passing through the detector gate. Everyone was taking off their belts in a haste and tried to move forward. The humming of people blended into the confusion inside him. He took his check-in card and passport out of his pocket. When he arrived at the Turkish Airlines desk, the attendant told him, "We can get your hand luggage if you like," and he replied, "No, thanks." Although he hurried to the gate, he saw that the Istanbul flight had not started to accept any passengers for boarding. Suddenly, he went back to the café he left behind and asked for water. When he grabbed the bottle of water, he suddenly had a bad feeling. Immediately, he recovered, took control of that feeling and heard the call for boarding the Istanbul plane. Drinking water, he walked slowly to the gate. He could see in people's faces that they were happy for being able to travel comfortably due to the affordability of flight prices. "I still prefer the train ride," he said to himself.

As he sat down in his seat, he noticed a tall, long-haired, hazel-eyed, white-skinned woman approaching him and checking the numbers with the corner of her eye. She stood next to Doruk, and after placing the small suitcase in the cabinet, "Can I?" she said. Doruk rose to his feet indifferently without a reply. She was rather beautiful and drew attention. Doruk's interest in her would only make Doruk ordinary.

"If a person is looking somewhere, there is something the person is interested in. If a person is not looking at a place at all, there is definitely something there that the person is interested in."

Freud

Doruk sat next to her and noticed that the woman was sitting on his seat belt. He moved his hand towards the seat belt. He slowly pulled the belt and the woman turned her head from the window towards Doruk and the aisle. Doruk said, "Sorry." This time she didn't reply. Doruk thought, "I'd better finish this character struggle and come up with something to meet her."

She had taken a few reminder cards out of her purse. He glimpsed at the sentences that were written on the cards. Each sentence was marked with a number. She crossed off a few. Doruk took an evasive glance at the cards. He saw some expressions like "Yılmaz Öztürk, additional statement for the court of appeals." The woman was apparently a lawyer and she had a long list of jobs. Doruk gave up looking at the cards from the corner of his eye and turned his head towards them. In return, she fixed her eyes on Doruk.

"I think you're a lawyer?"

"Yes."

"Can I get your opinion on something?"

"Yes."

"I presume you specialize in an area, don't you? Maybe it's not in your field."

"We have friends specialized in many different fields in our office."

"Well then, I work for the Ministry of National Defense as an engineer, and I have not been promoted although I was supposed to be a department head by now."

"Any disciplinary action against you etc.?"

"No, my record grades are very high."

"If you file a lawsuit within sixty days after your petition is turned down, you may have a chance depending on the information in your personal file. Of course, it is not easy. You have to fight."

"How long do you think it would take? By the way, I'm Doruk."

"The court rules for the termination of execution in about one and a half months, the appeal results in 2 to 3 weeks, then the court decides on the merits in six months to one year, finally the party that loses goes to the court of appeals, but I cannot give a definite timeframe for the appeal process. And I'm Filiz. Nice to meet you."

"Do you work in Ankara? Where is your office?"

"I work in Ankara and my office is in Kavaklidere. I occasionally travel to Istanbul for hearings. What about you?"

"I am also in Ankara. If I can get your business card, I'd like to come and visit you at your office to discuss this in detail."

Filiz got one of the cards sitting in the side pocket of her purse and handed it to Doruk.

Madrid

Galina saw other passengers turning on their phones after the plane landed. She also turned on hers. Doruk had texted, "Welcome." Galina chose to send a kiss in response.

After taking her hand luggage from the cabin, she waited for the people passing by to allow her into the aisle. But the Russian tourists were so impatient that she easily surrendered herself to the likelihood of being the last passenger to get off the plane. At that moment, a little girl smiled at Galina and allowed her to step into the aisle. Galina thanked her. The child's mother said, "Aren't you supposed to say, 'you're welcome?'" The little girl repeated, "You're welcome." Galina turned her head with a smile and walked through the aisle to the exit door.

For the first time, she did not feel like she was going on a mission even though this was a mission. The only thing in her head was her pregnancy. It had been eight days since she took the test. She was counting the days.

She took a taxi and went to the hotel where she would meet Doruk. She looked at her watch when she arrived at the reception desk. Then she saw Doruk's face as she entered the room, she felt obliged to put on a smile. They hugged each other and started kissing.

Thinking that sexual intercourse could be detrimental in the later stages of pregnancy, she took Doruk towards the bed without wasting any time. After taking off Doruk's clothes, Galina said, "I'll take a quick shower." "Okay, but be really quick," responded Doruk.

When Galina came out of the shower, she threw her robe over the nightstand. They started making love. Galina was on his lap and looking into his eyes while he was about to ejaculate. Doruk closed his eyes and came inside her, absorbing and sucking her lips. Galina lay down next to Doruk. After catching his breath, Doruk started to tell how much he loved and missed her. The words Galina used to listen to so eagerly were now like the buzz of a fly to her. She was disgusted by everything now.

She did not let Doruk notice anything during their three-day long vacation. Everything was like the old times. His hugging, touching, kissing, looking into her eyes. The way he caressed her skin...

"As complexity increases, exact expressions lose their meaning, and meaningful expressions lose their certainty."

Lütfi Zade

But she tried so hard not to reveal the hatred disguised deep in her soul. She wanted to shout it out and destroy Doruk and ask him how he could have done such a thing to her so ruthlessly by trading her for his work. But she couldn't. At least for the time being!

"Unexpressed emotions will never die. They are buried alive and will come forth later in uglier ways."

Freud

Doruk asked, "Are you a bit tired? You seem to be lost in thoughts. What are you thinking about?" Galina merely said, "I feel a little tired."

She would not know for sure if Doruk was going to write that detail in his report. There was a fake e-mail address, its password and the name of the "recorded files folder" on the small piece of paper Doruk gave her. Galina closed her eyes as if saying "okay."

Galina had planned to pass on some insignificant information to stay in the game.

"My love, shall we walk around Puerto Der Sol[5] Square?"

"All right, sure."

Galina murmured, "You're going to need a lot of sun."

The hotel was pretty close to the square, so they walked there. It was very crowded due to the presence of great historic buildings.

They were slowly walking and trying to explore the area. Galina activated the device in her bag as they walked. It was a counter technical tracking device, and when it was turned on, it would emit sound waves to prevent listening with a laser microphone.

"Before I forget to say, I dreamed that I was pregnant the night before we came here," said Galina. Doruk replied, "I hope so, in the soonest time possible," using the words professionally worked on before.

The Turks attached great importance to dreams. They would tell each other their dreams and get them interpreted. Doruk's mind would probably be engaged in Galina's dream.

Galina continued to tamper with his mind: "Don't worry, the moment I get pregnant, I'll tell you at the speed of light."

> *"Even telling a person not to think about something increases the chances of the person's thinking about that thing."*
>
> **Wegner & Erber**

She made another move saying, "You wouldn't be angry if I told my mom first, would you?"

---

[5] Gate of the Sun

"We can solve the quality of a problem not by its complexity, but by the complexity of the thought it triggers."

Joseph O'Conner

Doruk asked, "Shouldn't you share it with the father of the baby first?"

When Doruk asked this question, he improvised so much that he was also amazed. He went way out of the question-answer patterns he had studied.

Galina responded, "Yes, of course."

"If you ask questions wholeheartedly, you will receive answers wholeheartedly."

Omaha

Doruk and Galina ate their meals, did some shopping and took photos of the historical buildings using their cell phones. The music of the street musicians was so pleasant that Galina wanted to record it.

They set out to see the Palacio Real de Madrid[6]. The palace was simply wonderful. They were exhausted towards the end of the evening and decided to go to the hotel to get some rest, only to fall asleep right away.

The next day they woke up and visited the Museo Municipal, Palacio de Cristal and some other touristic sites.

Madrid was one of the most beautiful cities in Europe and its people were very friendly and warm-blooded. It had been a beautiful trip, both Doruk and Galina liked the city. Three days had flown by in a blink of eye.

Moscow

Galina called Denis when she finished her work at the headquarters.

They agreed to meet in the evening.

When she met Denis, she directly said,

---

[6] The Royal Palace of Madrid

"I have an important idea about your business. You need to find a good criminal lawyer."

"My lawyer Yegor is a very well-known successful lawyer."

"So, can you totally trust him?"

"He is fond of money, so he charges a lot, but he does a good job, never sells you out and doesn't let you down."

"Make an appointment with him tomorrow and let's go together."

"Okay, I will. Come on, tell me about your idea."

"If I find out that you've missed me when we get home, then I will tell you."

"I've missed you, but I'm very tired, tell me a little about this idea, come on!"

"Let me improve it a little bit more, and maybe it would be better to evaluate it with your lawyer tomorrow."

"Okay then, go home and get some rest."

When she met with Denis the next day, Yegor, one of Moscow's famous lawyers, was with him.

"Yes, Mr. Yegor, I would like to work with you on an issue."

"Sure, I'd be honored."

"The issue we want to work on is not real, it will be entirely fiction."

"Hmm..."

"It will be structured as if it were real, and the indicted will be acquitted quickly."

"..."

"The fiction will shake the society, but it will not comply with the legal technique."

"If you can elaborate on it a little bit more."

"I want you to prepare an exemplary case. Let us have a rich businessman who lives with a very attractive woman. And the woman has a one-year old child from her previous relationship."

"Yes."

"Of course, the man's house will be adapted according to the fiction. The house will have two floors. The child will sleep upstairs or downstairs with the mother. The man cannot tolerate noise."

"Yes."

"So, the details will be thoroughly thought and well-plotted."

"One day, the woman will go to the police claiming that the rich businessman has sexually abused her baby, then she will hire a good lawyer and will try to destroy the man by taking the issue to the media."

"Hmm. And then...?"

"But there will be legal deficits in woman's statements and events."

"But in this case the man can be arrested immediately."

"There you will find the legal loopholes to enable his acquittal immediately without having him arrested."

"The woman will claim that someone has threatened her with killing her baby if she didn't do that, after the man is cleared in public."

"As far as I understand, Denis will be the rich businessman, right?"

"Yes, Mr. Yegor."

"This is a very dangerous game."

"I'm aware of that."

"So, what's the point here?"

"Denis had previously been slandered. He was never proven to be guilty. But there was a perception in the public that the crime was in a sense admitted by the party by not nominating him again."

"Unfortunately."

"Now we're going to prove that somebody is messing with Denis in a mean way, making precarious and unfounded claims. So, we will create a public opinion that he is a victim and save his reputation. We will engrave in public's memory that Denis is not a traitor according to the 'determination of evidence' principle and we will prove the new issue is also a slander. It is logical but difficult."

"Should we come up with a different scenario? Because the court is very likely to issue an immediate arrest order in child and infant abuse cases."

"You will set up the script in such a way that even when Denis goes to testify without you, he will logically prove that the incident is fictitious."

"Can you give me a week for that?"

"We are not in a hurry."

Ankara

Doruk wanted to work in the Anti-terror Department to get the revenge for his martyr father. He was sick and tired of dealing with the Russians, and Galina had worn him out.

He grabbed his cell phone while writing his petition for reassignment, googled the phrase "getting pregnant in a dream" and studied the related dream interpretations.

"Without knowing the force of words, it is impossible to know more."

Confucius

He finished writing the petition as he was thinking in the back of his mind whether Galina's dream could come true. He stood up quickly, sighed deeply and muttered to himself, "Should I see the doctor again to understand whether this injection is hundred percent effective? If such a thing happens, a child from a foreign service agent, I would be ruined. Everyone will make a mock of me saying 'the Russian son of a Turanist,'" he thought.

"People tend to dramatize and think of the worst to happen."

Aaron Temkin Beck

He took his phone again, entered the favorites section and searched. "Hello, what have you done? Any developments?" he asked. The answer didn't seem to please him. He sulked saying "Okay, I'm coming." He took his jacket from behind his seat and put it on looking at his father's picture on his desk, then pulled out a wipe from the drawer and dusted the frame out.

The next day at their meeting, it was reported that they were not able to break into the house of the Russians by any means. They thought that the couple living in the house were planning some covert operations. The couple's routines were analyzed in detail and then turned into a sequential presentation. Towards the end of the meeting, the supervisor's face registered a sour look. He was looking into everyone's eyes and everyone was trying to avoid his eye-contact. Suddenly, he fixed his eyes on Doruk and said:

"Drop all your work and just focus on this issue. We need at least one device installed in here. We can't listen inside because of the high-tech wall."

"Should we try to place devices on the people living in this house?"

"It's too risky."

"Find a way of getting it done."

"Think carefully."

"Got it."

"If we try to put a microphone on those who enter the house, the entire operation will be ruined if it is understood during the placement."

Doruk took the file in his hand after the meeting. He read it multiple times and decided to do the same things that the people living in the house did during the day. When he explained this idea to his supervisor, the supervisor said they should feed him with instant information so that he would be able to do this unremittingly.

In the morning, after the couple left the house, Doruk drove through the same street and followed the same roads and routes to the couple's business premises by car. Anatoly was going to his office right after leaving Aleksandra to her work.

Doruk went all the way along the routes they used for twelve days, the restaurants where they ate, places they went shopping, friends they visited, bars they went to have fun, spa center, and the barber shop where Anatoly had his haircut. He also had a female officer go to the hairdresser where Aleksandra went every Monday morning to have a blow-dry.

He took photos of these places and studied all the photos and the people they saw repeatedly on his computer. But he could not find a way out.

From the wiretap, they got the information that the couple would attend the coffee festival on Sunday. Doruk quickly got up and went to the festival venue. Stands were already installed in the area. He only had half a day to do something. He approached the booth area and noticed a staff with a name tag. He immediately started to chat with her:

"Hi, is it too late to rent a booth?"

"Unfortunately."

"Hmm."

"Our stands were rented weeks ago."

"The promotion will last two days, right?"

"Yes."

"Will there be events, competitions etc.?"

"Several brands will distribute their coffee and cups free of charge."

"Great, I wish we had acted earlier."

The girl kept smiling.

"Well, which brands will distribute promotions? Let me come informed so that I won't return without a gift at least."

"Look at those two big stands across the street."

"Much obliged, see you again."

Doruk walked away and immediately returned to his office to look for information about the two companies. The share structure of one of the two companies was completely local. The other company mostly belonged to foreigners. He quickly shared his plan with his supervisor.

On Saturday, Anatoly called his colleague Nikolai. "I feel tired today. How about going to the coffee festival tomorrow?" he asked. "Okay, is tomorrow 12:00 pm good for you?" asked

Nikolai. Anatoly replied, "Fine, we'll meet where tickets are sold at the entrance."

The deciphering of the dialogue was quickly transmitted to Doruk.

Saturday evening, the identity information of the students working at the festival area was checked by the disguised social security officials at the entrance, nothing was found. The students were employed by the organization company whenever there was an event. Their background, parents and telephone contacts were quickly checked, and it was investigated whether they had any prior records at the Ministry of Interior. The students came up clean. That same evening, Ayşe, the youngest employee of the service, would meet with the girls and convince them. In addition, a promotional gift with a receiver inside would be given in an elegant box to the person they had identified, saying that they were giving a promotional trophy to every 50th person.

The day had come. Anatoly and Nikolai met. They joined the entrance queue. It was lively all around. Children riding scooters, teenagers and everyone had met at the festival. As most of the participants paid the entrance fee by credit card, the queue moved very slowly. E-mail addresses and mobile phone information were also required in addition to the entrance fee. A password confirmation was sent to either of these channels to allow the entry to the festival area. In this way, the festival organizers were creating a portfolio for advertising and future campaigns.

Ayşe was wearing the same clothes as the staff at the entrance. When Anatoly and Nikolai got in line, she stood next to the entrance staff and gave the trophy to them. Anatoly received the cup happily but gave it to Nikolai. Doruk muttered, "The gift exchange culture of the Russians."

It was time for plan B. Anatoly and Nikolai were walking around the stands slowly. Souvenirs, earrings and scarves were also sold at the coffee festival. The designers of small souvenirs and homemade items had printed their Instagram addresses on their cards and were distributing them to people who were not shopping.

When they came by the booth with seats in front of it, Anatoly and Nikolai had muffin and coffee. Then they stood up and walked up to the booth of the local firm. In the meantime, Doruk took his hand to his hair and acted as if he were arranging it. Standing at the booth, Bilge approached Anatoly and Nikolai with plastic bags in her hand. "Welcome, these are our promotional products," she said, holding out one bag for each. Nikolai took the bag. Anatoly asked, "What's in the bag?" "Coffee and a cup," replied Bilge. "Is it Turkish coffee?" inquired Anatoly. Bilge said, "Yes." Anatoly turned down the bag, "I'm not that much into Turkish coffee." Bilge went back to her seat without showing any reaction.

Doruk said to himself, "It is clear that the man consciously does not accept anything given to him by a stranger."

It was unusual of Doruk to return to the office demoralized. He went into his supervisor's room and told him about the incident. The supervisor responded, "All the politicians of the former Soviet geography are the same; they never get anything handed to them. Even when they do, they don't eat, drink, or use it but just throw it into a bin." His supervisor did not seem surprised at all, but apparently, he had wanted to try the method just in case.

The best solution was to duplicate the buttons of his clothes in the locker room while he was in the spa and place bugs in them. But Anatoly usually wore a shirt. The brand of his jeans he wore during the weekend was not clear and it was hard to determine because of the belt. He wondered whether he should place the bug in the belt. This time he could understand that the belt had been changed due to the marks caused by wearing out. They were probably checking their clothes electronically when they got into the house.

He decided to continue doing the same thing for several weeks until he found a solution.

Doruk was tired and bored now.

It was the first day of the month. Anatoly went to the bank within walking distance of his office to withdraw his salary and send money to his family.

An hour later, Doruk also went to the bank. The bank was very crowded when Anatoly got there around 11:45 am. Doruk got there right after lunchbreak and people were just coming in. He used the same bank's credit card so he would pay his credit card debt and see the atmosphere inside. Doruk took a number slip and started to wait. There were five or six people waiting for the teller's window. Although there were four windows, only three of them were functional.

When it was his turn, he greeted the teller and said,

"I want to pay my credit card debt."

"You can pay your card debt at the ATM outside."

"Can't I pay it here?"

"You can, but we usually refer our customers to the ATM. Well, let me get it."

"How much do I owe?"

"3.300 Liras."

"Okay, let's take it from my account and pay the debt."

"Sure."

"Could you sign here to withdraw money from your account, please?"

"Sure."

"Could you also sign here, this is the statement which shows that you have paid the card debt."

"Okay, let me sign. Thank you so much."

"You're welcome."

"May it be easy," he said to the security guard and walked towards the exit door. As he just got out of the door, he quickly turned around and walked over to the bank teller. "I'm sorry I got your pen, although it is written 'DO NOT' on the yellow post-it on the counter." The teller said, "Despite this notice, people take them by habit, and we have to buy boxes of pen." Doruk's eyes sparkled when he heard the teller say this. The teller could not understand why he was so happy as Doruk left the bank saying, "You are right, have a good one!"

He quickly picked up his phone, called his supervisor and asked, "Are you in the office?" The supervisor said, "I'm out," and asked, "Is it urgent?" "Not really, but I think I found a way that I want to share with you."

When he met his supervisor, he shared his idea:

"Let's put pens with bugs in the bank so Anatoly can habitually put them in his shirt pocket."

"Yes, it is possible, but it looks too difficult. Can't you find a way that is easier and more likely?"

"This is the least risky method, but the probability is very low, of course," he replied.

"Let's design the pen so that it has a strap that can be attached to the pocket. And let's have the bank logo on it."

"Okay."

"Of course, we should investigate the bank employees thoroughly."

"Sure."

Doruk studied the bank employees and prepared his report. After getting approval, he decided to see the branch manager in order to meet with all the bank tellers.

"Don't see the branch manager and the tellers yourself. She can recognize your face and try to find out your name. She may already identify you from the picture because your identity card has already been scanned during the bank transaction. Have someone else do the talks with the bank."

"Yes, it would be more appropriate."

"If we place the pens randomly and every customer gets one pen, the cost will increase."

"Yes, we'd better investigate the dates when he goes to the bank."

"Investigate it and find out if the bank teller has the chance to direct the person, he chooses to his transaction window."

"All right."

"But this can be risky, and if his turn comes up suddenly, maybe he may behave in a controlled way."

"Then, let's investigate whether the target usually goes to the bank when he receives bonus from the company, when he receives his salary or when his family demands money."

"It makes sense."

"Let's put the same pen at all teller windows."

"Yes."

"In fact, let's get the pens made in large numbers. If someone gets one and takes it away, our people can replace it."

"Yes."

"Anything else?"

"And, do not forget to tell them that the pens are bugged and that they are only for obtaining fingerprints. Don't go into much detail because if they realize that the job is very important, they might get excited and compromise the job."

He went to his room and grabbed his phone. "Let me call the lawyer," he murmured.

Doruk got the phone in his hand.

"Hello."

"How are you, bro?"

"I'm fine, how about you?"

"I'm fine too."

"You have lately mentioned that we were going to change our lawyer remember?"

"Yes, we were quite busy and could not look into it yet."

"I met a lawyer by chance."

"Let me guess, a beautiful woman?"

"Yes, I'll call her now and make an appointment."

"Okay."

"Are you available tomorrow?"

"I'll go to the Highways Directorate in the morning. Other than that, I'll be in the office."

"We'll talk tomorrow then. Take the file you were talking about with you so we can create a serious appearance."

"I will, don't worry."

Doruk dialed Filiz's number.

"Hello?"

"Ms. Filiz, how are you?"

"Fine, and you?"

"I'm fine too. If you're in the office tomorrow, I would like to visit you with a friend of mine. He has a legal case and is not happy with his current lawyer."

"Okay, I have a hearing before noon. How about sometime around 2: 30-3: 00 pm? "

"That would be fine."

"Well, see you then."

"See you."

The next day Doruk met with his friend Oğuz, and they went to Filiz's office. There was a little rush in the office when they entered. Doruk said, "I think we are disturbing Ms. Filiz on a busy day." "No inconvenience at all, please, it's just the routine rush of every day," she replied. Pointing to Oğuz, Doruk said, "This is my friend, Oğuz." Filiz shook hands with Doruk and then Oğuz. "Shall we drink Turkish coffee?" asked Filiz. Oğuz said, "I'll get mine without sugar." "The same for me," said Doruk. Filiz laughed saying, "Mr. Doruk, I'm currently looking into personal development, so let me just say that the phrase 'the same' is one of the forbidden phrases." "Then I'll take it plain too," he said smiling, "And why is it forbidden?" he asked. Filiz replied, "Because it's a phrase that prevents people from expressing themselves." "I've never thought about it from that perspective," he said. Oğuz added, "It's really interesting," and continued, "I'm the coordinator of a construction company and we have a lot of cases, but we don't think our lawyer is paying enough attention to our cases." "How did you reach this conclusion?" asked Filiz. Oğuz said, "Our petitions and cases are usually processed on the last day, and we are losing time. He doesn't seem committed."

After about 10 minutes of conversation, Filiz put her hands on the armrests of her seat and said, "E-mail me the file you're talking about and I'll get back to you right after I review it."

Just as Doruk and Oğuz were going to walk out of the door thanking her, Doruk said, "Ms. Filiz, when you get a chance, could you please send me some personal development book names so I can do some reading?" Filiz replied, "Of course I can, and I can even send the ones I couldn't read yet, and you can tell me what is important in them. " Doruk said, "Agreed, if the word is not 'banned.'" Filiz smiled, "No, it's not."

Moscow

A Few Weeks Later

When Galina and Denis arrived at Yegor's office, his secretary said, "Mr. Yegor's meeting will end in a few minutes. Please have a seat."

Galina and Denis took their seats and started to wait for Yegor.

Yegor's secretary picked up the phone and called Yegor, "Mr. Denis and his guest are waiting to see you," and she hung up.

Before meeting with Denis, Galina made sure to wear loose clothes that did not reveal her bodylines. She didn't know how Denis would react to the idea of a baby and she was worried. He was in depression and could go violent against her while he was drunk, causing her to lose the baby. From now on she was going to live only for her child. She wanted to be a mother. Who wouldn't?

In a few minutes, Yegor's interview ended and the crowd left his office. The secretary invited them saying, "This way please. Mr Yegor is ready to see you."

When they went into the office, Galina told Yegor, "Your office is very stylish." Yegor replied, "Thank you. Most of the objects are antiques."

Denis intervened, "Yegor is not only a good lawyer but also an antiquarian with a high taste."

Galina said, "I absolutely agree."

Denis told Yegor, "You seem to have looked into the matter, Yegor."

Yegor replied, "I did my research to turn you into a hero and I can brief you. Because of the confidentiality of the matter, I personally did the design and research. Even the lawyers in my office have no idea about this.

Galina said, "Very appropriate."

Denis added, "Absolutely, now tell us about it."

"So, the woman you are going to find must be very discreet, play her role very well, should only answer the questions, be well-educated or capable of being educated," Yegor explained.

Denis said, "Yes, she will share the lead role indeed."

Yegor asked, "I guess your house is suitable for our design. You still live in the same house, don't you?"

Denis replied, "Yeah."

Yegor inquired, "And is there a man in your neighborhood who lives with a woman who has both money and has just given birth?"

Denis, "Not to my knowledge."

Galina asked, "But there is no obstacle or law to prevent it from happening, is there?"

Yegor said, "Yes, but it doesn't attract attention, I hope. I got a little stuck in this part."

Galina said, "I think it's okay, as long as she's beautiful."

Yegor continued, "So, here is the game plan. Your lover will say that you rubbed your genitals on the baby, and before that you held the baby in your lap a few times, but she thought it might be normal."

Galina asked, "And then?"

Yegor went on, "The next day Denis will leave the town for a week. And she will file a complaint about Denis a week later."

Denis asked, "Do we need any witnesses?"

Yegor replied, "No, that would make our job difficult."

Galina confirmed him, "I agree."

Yegor said, "This claim is hard to prove because it is not a rape charge."

"Yes, in fact this is the most relaxing part for me," said Denis.

Yegor continued to tell, "The subtlety here is that the woman will file her complaint after the reasonable timeframe. Your being out of town for a week and the fact that she files her complaint about the same day you come back even before you get home will make people think that the woman is slandering you out of jealousy as she had some suspicions about the presence of another woman. But when evaluating sexual harassment, the Russian Federation Supreme Court of Appeals takes into account various factors such as whether the location of the incident is suitable for the complaint, the nature of the incident, that is, the intensity of the action and the extent of the reaction of the plaintiff or victim, who is too young to place a complaint, and the timing of the complaint."

"So, it will be important that she is late in terms of complaining and she hasn't attacked me," Denis responded.

Yegor approved.

Galina asked, "Do you have a few examples of these court decisions that I can read?"

Yegor said, "Yes, here you are. I already wanted to show you. That'll do it if you just read the underlined parts."

"Yes, the court has set some criteria here," said Galina.

Denis was curious, "What are those criteria?"

Galina counted, "Immediate complaint, immediate reaction, counterattack, fighting back..."

Yegor added, "Other than that, there are criteria whether the event complies with the normal course of life and so on."

Denis commented, "So, when they take me to the police station, I will claim that the incident is a slander and I will defend myself asking, 'Why didn't she complain immediately, why didn't she attack me, why didn't she leave the house after a week?'"

Yegor said, "Exactly."

Denis was not sure, "That's nice, but do you think it's risky anyway?"

Yegor explained, "We will focus on details such as who will be in charge at the police station and which prosecutor will be on duty on the day of the complaint. We will start the game as soon as I make these arrangements."

"Very good, I hope we can handle it smoothly. What if you can't set it up at the center?" asked Galina.

Yegor replied, "In that case, we can devise another plan."

Galina said, "You mean another location and a police station affiliated with that location?"

Yegor confirmed, "Yeah."

"That's good," responded Galina.

Yegor kept explaining, "After you give your testimony, you will complain against the woman for slander, and you will claim that the second phase of the trap was set and that you were labelled a terrorist in order to prevent your candidacy. Before you testify, you'll want the statement to be recorded on camera."

Denis said, "Yes, it can be a nice PR."

Yegor added, "Yes, but not only that. This will also reveal your level of comfort to the prosecutor when the file is transferred to him."

Galina said, "We will also give it to the media."

"Yes, we will do that, too," confirmed Yegor.

Galina added, "While all this is going on, it would be nice if you get separated from the woman and get married to a woman you used to know."

> *"The smartest way to get out of some situations is to infect others with our own feelings."*
>
> **Kafka**

Denis said, "Yes, I never thought of that."

Yegor agreed, "It would be great. We also need to find this."

Galina continued, "If we do this, the public will think that if Denis were really that kind of a man, the woman he used to know would not marry her. And that would be great."

Denis said, "Yes, it would be great, but first we need to get rid of this situation before I am arrested. So, Yegor, in the meantime, would it be useful if the woman withdrew the complaint before I get married and even confessed to slandering me?"

Yegor said, "Nobody confesses to slander. Because the slanderer may face imprisonment. But, even though her withdrawal from the complaint might be useful, the file won't get closed since this crime concerns the general public."

Galina came up with another idea, "If the woman you marry has just given birth to a baby, that would be much better."

Yegor agreed, "That would be great. If we can achieve this, you will be completely cleared in the public eye."

Denis said, "Yes, it would be great. But what if we make a mess of everything?"

Galina assured him, "It seems like there will be no problem if we find someone we really trust and study everything in detail."

"Yes, then we could be subject to blackmail. We have to choose our players well," said Yegor.

Denis asked, "Can you give me a risk estimate?"

"five percent," replied Yegor.

Galina was optimistic, "If we work hard, we can minimize the risk."

Denis said, "So everything will work out this way?"

Galina explained, "Denis, both the mother and the child will certainly make the papers, and you will have to pay them the cost of changing their names, otherwise we will devastate the future of the child."

"No problem," said Denis.

Yegor continued, "We will pick one of the women who have been fired from the model agencies due to drug abuse."

Denis said, "It makes sense."

Galina wasn't so sure, "We can't trust a drug addict!"

Yegor was thinking, "Hmm ..."

Galina added, "It can be a woman who left the agency for a reason other than drugs."

Denis interjected, "It shouldn't be too hard to find a woman who has quitted her job to get married while she's pregnant but has been abandoned and is in need of money."

Yegor agreed, "Yes, this has already become a national tradition in Moscow!"

Galina told them, "I'm going to look for a woman personally, and we shouldn't limit ourselves to only model agencies. But the woman we're going to find should be beautiful because if Denis appears in the media with an ugly woman, this might have negative consequences for PR."

"Bravo Galina!" exclaimed Denis.

*

Inga showed the news article about an American citizen woman who told about what she had experienced in an ISIS camp. The interview had taken place in Netherlands. She asked Galina if her story was true. Galina scanned the article.

The title of the article read: "The True Face of ISIS." It continued: "She told about her experiences in the large camp set up in the city captured by ISIS: 'What I experienced in the camp was horrible. I witnessed many atrocities. Islam is not practiced in the camp; they have a catalog of the skin color of women in their hands, and they force women to get married according to this catalog. There is no trace of Islam in the camp and I never saw anyone reading the Koran properly. I was married to a member of the War Council, Abu Mahmoud, for almost a year. He was not a Muslim. But he was pretending to be a Muslim. I will share more information with the public once I recover myself.'"

Looking at Inga,

Galina said, "Very interesting information."

"I agree. Do you think it is true?"

"It could be, do you?"

"There are also similar claims about their leaders."

"In the Muslim-looking terrorist organizations, the selection of women from the catalog didn't seem unfamiliar to me."

"Really? What organization was that?"

"Which one was it?... Now I remember! The CIA's Fetullah branch!"

"Well, all right?"

"They were active in the Crimea."

"Right..."

Although ISIS, aka DAES, did not fall within the realm of the Americans' Office, it was interesting that Inga had Galina read the story and received her opinion. A voice from inside Galina told her that even if they had a great professional accomplishment as a team, she should be careful about her. It would be hard to keep her guard against a person with whom she was always together.

"We don't see things around us as they are,
we see them as we are."

Anais Nin

Inga was very upset. Galina asked, "What's wrong with you? Is everything okay?" showing interest in her. Inga's reply was, "Not bad."

"What's up? As far as I understand, you have a problem with Grigory?"

"I don't know why, but he treats me bad for some reason."

"Come on, Inga, he must have a reason."

"He's been choking me with work lately as if trying to punish me."

"Could it be because he trusts you?"

"I don't think so."

"So, why then?"

"It is possible that he wants to get rid of me."

"He could do that easily if he wanted to."

"I guess you are right. But what's the problem then?"

"Could it be that he wants you?"

"I don't think so. He would have said that clearly if he wanted to."

"Sure?"

"Yes."

"Should we go out for a drink in the evening?"

"Sure."

"There's a place I've been to several times. It also has a separate Karaoke section inside. We will let off some steam."

"That'd be great."

"You're going home when you get out of here?"

"Yes."

"How about you?"

"I'll do the work that Grigory assigned to me."

"What time do we leave?"

"I'll come and pick you up at 11:30 pm."

"Okay, see you."

When Inga got in the car, Galina noticed she looked tired.

"Have you finished the work?"

"No, not until next week."

"You look very chic."

"So, do you!"

"I put on whatever I could find in the closet at work."

"Are you sure you're coming from work?"

"Why did you ask?"

"I smell some alcohol," she said smiling,

"I apparently forgot to mention the bar I stopped by on the way."

"I haven't been to a karaoke bar for a long time."

"It's the right place to relieve stress."

"Absolutely."

Interestingly, Inga had invited Galina to her home the previous week and they had a long conversation then. And this time she invited Inga out for the night.

Galina recalled what she had told at Inga's house last week:

"Inga, you've never told about yourself."

"Well, my story is a bit interesting and long."

"I'm all ears."

"Back in my childhood, when I was about four or five, my mother began to teach me how to play the piano."

"Was your mother a pianist?"

"No, a singing trainer."

"Very nice."

"My first teacher was my mother. I've played the piano for as long as I can remember myself."

Galina suddenly paused when she got this answer, for she could now relate this information well. Inga constantly used words pertaining to the sense of hearing such as "The man's voice was great", "the car made such a disgusting sound", "you can't imagine how I listened to it", "I did a voice analysis of our target on YouTube", "The holes in the sides of the barrel of the gun made the sound terrible", "It sounds terrible." Her large and long earlobes were a good manifestation of this as well.

"What did your father do?"

"My father wasn't a musician, but he was a good listener and he never got bored with the sound of music at home. My mother was a tough woman though. We lived together as a family for a long time, and then they got divorced and my father married someone else."

"I went to a school for music education between the ages of seven and fourteen and attended the Fine Arts High School Music Department between the ages of fourteen and eighteen. Then I went to the Conservatory. The first piano type I started playing was upright Riga. It was hard to be admitted to music high school back then. Of the two hundred and fifty applicants, they only received fifteen. I was the best at what I was doing. But I was very emotional about piano. Making music was important to me. I never wanted to be a soloist, either. But I'm a great companion. I feel all the choir, breaths and music while playing. I feel happiness when we get the desired results."

"Isn't it very difficult to play the piano?"

"Yes, it is a very difficult instrument, but thanks to my mother's discipline, I became a pianist."

"You mean lots of crying?"

"I never cried, but there were times when I practiced in anger. There was a contest when I was about eight or nine years old. My mother really wanted me to participate and she would wake me up at night asking questions about the series."

"Interesting."

"Yes, my mother was a very authoritarian woman. My brother wasn't talented. That's why my mother chose me as the victim in the family."

"What was the result of the contest?"

"Of course, I won the first place. My mother started with half an hour a day from the day she realized my finger technique was innate. I was working 4 hours a day to get ready for the competition. I would routinely go to school in the morning and come back home around 2:00 in the afternoon. After I finished my homework, I would start practicing the piano. I mean, I used to work until 9:00 in the evening."

"What a great determination!"

"Yes, I was very grateful to my mother, though she had chosen me as the piano victim."

"Grateful?"

"I'll tell you..."

"All right."

"I was a natural. A person is either an artist by birth or not. There are two types of people: artists and others. As long as I've known myself, I've never dreamed of a goal except for being a pianist. It was like I was born to be a pianist. That was the way my mother showed me, even though she forced me."

"So, why did you get into the Service?"

"I'm coming to that point."

"Okay."

"Bach has always been the artist I respect the most."

"Absolutely a wonderful artist."

"Yes, he figured out the mathematics of music very well, he is the genius of music. But there is only one work that I'm really in love with and it's Rachmaninoff's Piano Concerto. No. 2."

"It must be called love at first hearing, not love at first sight?"

"Exactly, I was in my second year of high school, getting ready for a contest. My teacher had given me another concerto. I was just passing by a door and I suddenly froze where I was. What I heard there had triggered such deep feelings in me that I could not describe. 'I have to find out immediately who this work belongs to,' I said to myself. I did a lot of research on the emotions and meanings hidden in the composition. This concerto could only be played by a conservatory student at her 20s. During the preparation stage for the contest, my teacher asked me how I was doing?"

"Weren't you already prepared?"

"I said no, but when I said no, I felt blushed. The teacher was very temperamental and disciplined."

"What did he say?"

"I was very surprised that he didn't get angry at all. 'And what is it that you want?' he asked."

"You said Rachmaninoff, I assume."

"Yes, I wanted the Concerto No. 2. I was baffled when he said 'then you will come here and play the 2nd part tomorrow morning at 08:30. How was I supposed to play a piece the notes of which I was yet to decipher. I had about fifteen hours ahead of me. How could I do that? Setting the appointment at 8:30 in the morning was on purpose so that I wouldn't be able to get ready."

"I suppose you did it?"

"Yes, I did."

"Did your mother help you in the meantime?"

"At the time I was working alone but my mother had always trained me. My mother usually played a piece and wanted me to write the solfège. I already had the absolute pitch."

"Absolute?"

"I mean I could figure out the note of the sound when you hit a blackboard with a pen in your hand."

"Amazing!"

"I was very curious about music, among other things. And I was very happy to solve the connection between mathematics of music and sensation."

"Your story is really great."

"Normally, people call themselves pianists at the conservatory level, but I had already been accepted as a pianist in high school."

"Although people started the piano with Hanon or Czerny – and I always studied them as I needed them in the exams- I always listened to Bach and tried to decipher his works. To me, Bach is the father of this field, he does music with math, and there is no such a brain all over the world," she said in excitement. "I had spent sixteen years of my life with music and art in this way."

"Were you giving concerts?"

"I gave my first concert in 4th grade. I also gave concerts in tournaments. I appeared at my first serious concert with the Almaty Philharmonic Orchestra at the age of fifteen. The piece I performed there was Rachmaninoff's Piano Concerto No. 2."

"Have you ever had a pianist lover?"

"Yes, I have. We met in high school. He was a year older than me. He was a great pianist who impressed me with his talent and was a great composer. Now he is in Europe."

"The saying 'music is the food for the soul' is true, isn't it?"

"Yes, the best anti-depressant for me is the piano. It gives me energy, I try to decipher very difficult pieces when I am emotional, and I feel satisfied to overcome that difficulty."

"You never wandered around, apparently?"

"Conservatory training was very intensive, 9 hours a day. I was also giving private lessons on weekends. I would hang out at night with the money I earned and enjoyed a high-quality night life. We were going to nightclubs that played quality music. The money my parents sent me and what I earned was not enough though. I couldn't cook because I had no time for that, so I would eat out. Money was draining fast like water."

"Were you staying with your family when you studied at the conservatory?"

"At that time my parents had moved to another city. I was staying in the dorm, in a room for three. One person had left the room. My roommate was a music theoretician. We got along very well. She was a lesbian and started to get very jealous of me."

"I can't believe it."

"She seemed to be in love with me, then we had a short relationship."

"Very exciting, and then?"

"Then we broke up."

"Were the lessons and exams difficult in the conservatory?"

"The exams took place over the course of two semesters. Each semester there was a jury of five to six teachers, and you were required to prepare a program. This program consisted of a sonata and a concerto. We decided on the works to be played in these programs together with our advisers, but the final decision mostly belonged to the advisers."

"Did you ever get low grades? You were very successful though."

"During a jury, my adviser was sick. He was the one who had decided on the pieces of the program, so for the first time I got four out of five. It was traumatic, and I was angry with myself for a long time."

"What is your horoscope sign, Inga?"
"Taurus."
"So, you love hard things."

"Absolutely. Since I am a Taurus, hardship attracts me. I try harder and harder on difficult pieces; I have never failed to play a piece for which I challenged myself. I love the challenge. I can't stand people who are not smart and talented."

"Was there a course you didn't like?"

"The courses are actually about teachers, for example, the Analysis of Music Form course was a ridiculous high school course for me. I had memorized it all until the morning. He was a teacher trying to limit music to patterns and wanted the students to memorize them. Apart from that, we also had teachers who rubbed their hands on our necks and backs and said that we did not sweat enough, meaning that we weren't working with all our feelings and strength."

"Great to listen to your story!"

"A little different story."

"I guess you won't tell the mom and the service part?"

"Let me tell you," she said reluctantly.

"I'm listening."

"My mother sent me to Moscow in the summer of my senior high school year. I had to finish high school in Russia in order to study at the Conservatory in Moscow. I knew there was a famous high school in Moscow. I went there and met the teachers. I played a few pieces. They liked it very much and invited me to take a test at the end of the summer. I took the test and returned home before the announcement of the results. I had given my aunt's number to school. I was reminding my mom to call my aunt every day. Mom was saying they hadn't called. Then the day came when my aunt became very sick. My mother and I went to Moscow. My aunt looked really bad. I was deeply crushed to see the person whom I considered my light of hope in such a condition. While we were talking about this and that, she said that she couldn't make sense of why I didn't come even though I was invited to the high school." When Inga said the last sentence, she seemed to be living that moment again.

Galina couldn't find anything to say. She just gulped and tried to look at Inga with compassion.

"I was frozen. I couldn't move for a few minutes. Then I immediately put on my shoes and left. My mother had changed the course of my life...I had tried to please her all my life. I was like a soldier. I was getting up the time she wanted me to and kept working, working and working."

"You are right."

"My mother hated my father's profession."

"What did he do?"

"He was working for the KGB. I had done what my mother wanted for years."

"So, you did what your father wanted? Or what you yourself wanted?"

"My purpose in doing so was actually taking revenge on my mother by not doing what she wanted, that is, quitting the piano. And then working at the job that she hated the most. "

"Hmm, rebellion…Spiritual revolt…"

"Yes. I was the toy of a literally narcissistic mother…"

> *"They might direct a complete affection of an object to the child whom they have given birth to and they see as a part of their own body just like an outer object aimed by their own narcissism."*
>
> **Sigmund Freud**

> *"Since the mother regards the child as a part of herself, she satisfies her own narcissism with love and extreme indulgence in her child."*
>
> **Erich Fromm**

> *"Childlike affection of parents is a manifestation of their own narcissism in the form of affection for an object."*
>
> **Sigmund Freud**

"Hmm..."

"My mother had a narcissistic personality disorder, as I understood it. For her, life was just about herself; other people's thoughts, wishes including those of mine did not matter. She couldn't be a pianist."

"Why not?"

"Those who get piano training from singing trainers cannot be as successful as a pianist who takes a professional training in terms of hand technique and position. As she wasn't able to become a professional pianist, she wanted me to become one."

> *"The child will realize their parents' desirous dreams which have never been materialized."*
>
> **Sigmund Freud**

"Hmm... I was with a narcissist when I was in college. Narcissists have no feelings. It was too late when I realized that. You are right in quitting music. So, are you happy with this career?"

"I am."

"Your mother didn't commit suicide when you quitted the piano, did she?"

"She was too narcissistic to commit suicide," she said and got up, "I quickly need to go to the restroom."

Galina said to herself, "She seems upset."

Inga entered the room walking slowly.

"So, where were we?"

"We were talking about your mother and aunt."

"Oh. Yes. After meeting with my aunt, I focused on my mom for days and thought about my mother's relationship with other people. I even noted down some events on paper and evaluated my mother's behavior in all of them."

"What conclusion did you reach?"

"I came to the conclusion that she didn't really like people."

> *"... The loving mother can only and truly be a loving mother when she has the capability to love and when she can love her husband, other children, strangers and all people."*
>
> **Erich Fromm**

"So, your mother hadn't sent you because of her ego and just because she wanted it that way, not because you were young and would have difficulty to succeed?"

"Yes."

> *"... The child is a natural object that is very conducive to a woman who loves to be superior and enjoys possession."*
>
> **Erich Fromm**

"Hmm."

"By not sending me to Moscow, my mother had shown me that she didn't want my happiness."

> *"Mother's love requires the ability to give everything and not to want anything other than the happiness of the loved one."*
>
> **Erich Fromm**

"Hmm."

"My mother did not think that I would leave her like every other child when the day came, and she had not prepared herself for it."

> *"Half of the mother's life should be filled by the desire for the child to be independent and eventually to separate the child from herself."*
>
> **Erich Fromm**

"Hmm."

"Except for the piano, I have no memories with my mother. The mothers of my school friends were lovely. I was always jealous of them."

"Don't you ever play the piano?"

"Every now and then, I do."

"And was your artistic spirit affected by this event?"

"I'm still an artist, just not performing!"

"And how did your father tolerate your mother?"

"My maternal grandfather was a senior officer at the MGB[7]"

In her mind Galina said to herself, "What a strong will it is, quitting the piano that she calls 'my soul' for revenge and then working in the service."

When they came in front of the club, she saw young people smoking outside. The bodyguards with dark beards at the entrance caught her attention. "The Chechens are in charge of the security of the place apparently," she murmured. As soon as they entered, they saw that there was a bar, a dance floor in front of the bar and a small elevated stage across the dance floor. When she turned her

---

[7] State Security Ministry - Ministerstva Gasudarstvennay Bezopasnosti

head to the left, she saw that a video clip was playing on a big screen on the wall. Everyone on the stage was trying to dance to the rhythm of the music. As they passed through the dancers, Inga reached out to Galina and they walked up the stairs. There were tables and armchairs upstairs, just like downstairs. They opened the glass door on which the word karaoke was diagonally written in large letters in order to enter the Karaoke section. When they came in, Inga called the waitress and whispered something in her ear. The waitress called the guest service attendant and pointed to the table with a reserve tag on it. Apparently, they had arrived late.

There was a Grigory Leps video clip on the screen. Two girls were singing the song "Samiy lutshi den."

Everyone was having fun. Inga had ordered champagne. When Inga asked Galina what she would drink, she replied, "Only tonic for now." Inga insisted, "Come on, let me order a glass for you, don't be a killjoy!" Galina said, "Okay, but tonic, too."

"I was going to ask something at home the other day, but I forgot to," said Galina. Inga asked, "So, what is it?"

"Who is your favorite author?"

"Tolstoy."

"Is it true that Tolstoy was a Muslim?"

"I've heard it, but I've never searched about it; you know I see the world through the window of art. 'Art has no religion.'"

"You are right."

When it was their turn to sing, Inga requested Irina Duptova's song "O Nem." She was very emotional when she sang the song. She pointed to Galina to stand up and join her. They were having fun. Galina was still on guard. She was always skeptical of Inga's rapprochement and efforts to build a bond with her. Perhaps she should have deepened this bond and even turned it into an opportunity. But why would she turn it into an opportunity? She wanted to get out of all these things. Therefore, she avoided the phrases used by the psychologist Ms. Yulya such as "I see, I promise to help you if you want it, etc." in order not to get closer to Inga.

Inga had something dangerous about her in terms of building a friendship. She had noticed that her colleagues were not close with her even though she started working in the Office of the Americans prior to herself. Everyone kept a distance with her.

When their songs were finished, the girls who stood up from the next table requested a song from "Okean Elzy" and started to sing in Ukrainian. When all the tables accompanied the song, Galina reacted in surprise saying, "Look at this! Everyone is so fond of Ukrainian; we must have fought against Bandera in vain."

"But it is art, after all."

"Even if it is art, Ukrainian nationalism has always been a threat."

"Art has no language."

"…"

"Galina, I admire your intelligence, I would have messed up with everything in Boston if it hadn't been for you. You were the only one who deserved to stand on the stage at the ceremony."

"One can defend himself against criticisms,
but he is powerless in the face of praise."

Freud

"Come on, Inga, we both deserved applause; if you hadn't deserved it, nobody would have rewarded you anyway."

Galina wasn't used to internal praise. Her instincts warned her to be careful.

Inga stood up and hugged the girls on the stage and accompanied the song. She looked very pleasant when she sat down. Looking into Galina's eyes, she said,

"I told you before that there was a general among my job references, but he wasn't actually a general, he was a deputy who was my boyfriend's father."

"Why did you say he was a general then?"

"Because I wanted to get him out of my head, I didn't pronounce his name or anything that would remind me of him."

"Good method."

"It definitely works."

"What's Tom doing now?"

"He got married, had two children, and then got divorced."

"Maybe you will make it up again."

"But I no longer have any feelings for him."

"Is there someone else then?"

"Yes."

"Who?"

"You probably don't know him."

"In Moscow?"

"Yes."

"Come on, tell me about it."

"Okay but promise me it'll stay between us."

"Promise."

"One of my sources."

"Wow!"

"Yes."

"But this is very dangerous."

"Yes, I don't write in my reports so it wouldn't be understood that some information is coming from him, and the man won't get into trouble."

"Inga, you're simply crazy."

"…"

The conversation went on.

Galina kept being precautious.

Inga acted as if she were transparent, having nothing to hide. By sharing her own private and sensitive information, she aimed Galina to share her secrets and mistakes, that is, to respond to the truthful relationship and openness between them.

Galina was aware that the sentences directed to her were in fact the questions with hidden purposes.

"See the sentence itself as a tool and its meaning as its purpose."

Ludwig Wittgenstein

"The solution to almost every problem is in the way it is formulated."

Jean Piaget

"Everyone has to predict the behavior of others, and that's why we all need theories about what drives people."

Steven Pinker

Galina was not naive enough to disclose her secrets to Inga!

"One immediately forgets the mistake he has confessed to another, but the other person does not easily forget it."

Nietzsche

So, Galina acted like a good listener and kept silent.

"Talking is a need, but silence is an art."

Germaine de Stael

"Silence is a ready-made answer that is too difficult to tolerate."

F. K. Chesterian

"Saying the right word can be effective, but no word can be as effective as silence with a correct timing."

Mark Twain

Inga was touching Galina's hand as she talked, creating an intimate atmosphere by increasing eye contact. Apparently, Inga was told to engage the weapon of sincerity and intelligence.

"The most effective weapon of people is sincerity and intelligence."

Halide Edip Adıvar

Inga was angry at Galina's silence. But she was trying not to show this feeling of hers. Coupled with what she told her at home, Galina was now supposed to feel comfortable and be ready to build an emotional connection with Inga. Inga thought, "Galina doesn't seem to drop her guard at all."

Galina was also considering whether to tell Grigory what Inga had told her. The purpose of Inga's narratives could be to see if Galina would relay the information she got from Inga. Therefore, telling Grigory what had happened would be the first thing to do tomorrow.

When they asked for the bill, Inga's eyes had already revealed that she needed some sleep. They paid the bill and stood up. After passing through the door to the Karaoke section, they slowly moved downstairs. While they were walking through the crowd, she held Galina's hand again. Galina looked at the stage and saw two female dancers waving their Black and White wings. "The Black Doruk," she murmured.

The next day she waited for Grigory to arrive. She could hardly sleep trying to figure out the motive behind Inga's behavior. Grigory was on the phone when she went to his room. "Come on in," he signed to Galina. Then he hung up and said, "Good morning."

"Good morning."

"Anything urgent?"

"It may not be urgent, but there's something you should know."

"So, what's up?"

"Last night, Inga told me that she had been having an affair with her American source and that she hadn't reported some information obtained from him in order to keep him away from trouble."

"Hmm…"

"Yes, she did tell all these, but I didn't understand why she told these to me."

"Okay, let's record their next meeting and see if she is withholding any information."

"Okay."

After Galina left the room, Grigory took his cell phone. He typed a short message to Inga, "Wrong guess!" And Inga typed, "not a guess but a hunch." She hesitated for a moment but then pushed the "send" button.

"You can think in the wrong way, you can misunderstand, you can do wrong, but you can't feel wrong."

La Edri

"The best weapon against an enemy is another enemy."

Friedrich Nietzsche

"Your chances of being killed by your loved ones are twice as likely as being killed by a stranger."

Charles Bukowski

"A man who is in control of his world can turn his pain into enthusiasm and his lack of love that creates depression into lasting love."

Tezer Özlü

"Being comes with a cost; everyone should learn it."

Shirley Abbott

"Actions are true to the extent that they tend to increase happiness, and false to the extent that they tend to produce the opposite of happiness."

J. S. Mill

*

Galina was questioning herself if she was sure she wanted to marry Denis? Could she live with him for the rest of her life?

"Ask yourself this question before you get married: 'Can I talk to this person for the rest of my life?' Everything else is temporary in marriage."

Nietzsche

"Love means finding the missing part in one's self."

Plato

Galina was going to have a child and had to leave the service. She wouldn't be able to live the way she wanted if she stayed. She was absolutely determined to leave.

"There is only one achievement, which is to live the way you want."

Christopher Morley

Was the purpose of Galina's plan to satisfy herself? Or was it because she fell in love with Doruk and she wanted to make sure that he wouldn't be with other women? In her unconscious Galina had the fixation that Doruk belonged to her. She was not sure whether Doruk belonged to her, but she could easily predict the consequences of what she was doing.

"The end can justify the means, as long as there is something to justify the end."

Trotsky

Galina wanted to kill Doruk based on her plan. She wondered if she had another purpose. She couldn't go after her heart anymore. Going by her heart would only mean her end. She had to act with her mind and logic. She could no longer live guided by her feelings only.

"Follow your heart but take your brain with you."

Alfred Adler

"If you have committed evil, fear! Because it is a seed. God will make it come into leaf and you will have to face it."

Rumi

She was going to meet Vladimir, Denis's best friend. After meeting Galina, Vladimir waited for her to go to the restroom in order to find answers to the questions that he couldn't make sense of. The moment had come, and Galina went to the bathroom. Vladimir quickly started talking:

"Denis, have you really made up your mind?"

"Yes."

"I think you should take your time. Just because she is helping you, you don't have to feel indebted and reward her by tying the knot."

"I have found the remaining half of me in her."

"Look, these stressful days will pass, maybe you'll get bored with her. You don't even know her properly..."

"Choosing a spouse is similar to selecting a book, a well-designed cover and binding may interest you, but it is difficult to finish it unless the content is solid."

Confucius

"I feel very good when I'm with her."

"People who make you feel good are addictive."

Erich Fromm

"Is feeling good enough by itself?"

"Maybe it's not enough alone, but I really want to marry her."

"There are better people around you. You should rethink your decision. Look around you; you got stuck in Galina, repeating her name like a broken record…"

"You should choose the one that makes you feel better, not the better one."

Erich Fromm

"I wasn't going to tell you this, but I fell in love with Galina."

"Marrying without loving is a vile thing to do just like worshiping without believing."

Chekhov

"You don't need to say it. It is clear as daylight. Do you think love will last forever?"

"It may not, but I enjoy spending time with her, I never get bored. So, no one will get married because love will end?"

"You're obsessed and you can't make a healthy decision; you must have been overwhelmed by the events. Do you need to rush this much? I don't want you to feel sorry later. Take some more time together. You're a politician and you can't marry someone out of the blue. And remember, there is also the divorce part of it!"

"Vovchik, I seriously questioned this decision, and I'm comfortable with it!"

"… On vital matters such as choice of spouse or profession, the decision comes from the unconscious, from within."

Freud

"Look, why don't you start seeing Luda again, and she is much prettier."

"I don't attach importance to beauty anymore. What I've been through has changed me a lot. I can't describe my feelings to you, but I'm sure you'll understand me as time goes by. I've also heard that Luda's Miss World title has been revoked due to drug abuse."

"A plain woman prefers being beautiful to being intelligent. Because a plain man does not have the brain to understand intelligence, but the eyes to see the beauty."

Anton Chekhov

"Don't change the subject."

"No, I don't."

"You should try it again with Luda. She called me recently, and we had a long chat."

"Luda can be strikingly beautiful, but there was something missing in her; we couldn't have enjoyable time together."

"One who enjoys what he owns is happy, not the one who owns the best of everything."

Vladimir Nabokov

"What would you lose if you got to know her a bit more?"

"Remember, true love blossoms as one gets to know the other."

Erich Fromm

*

Galina muttered to herself, "The biological father of my child is Denis, but you are the mental father."

"Fear not, I will take you not by force but in my heart and mind."

Halide Edip Adıvar

Galina took it personally what she lived with Doruk. After all, they were both secret service agents. She thought what happened to her was Doruk's personal preference. She couldn't keep this emotion away from her head.

"The problem is not that they could not see the solution but that they could not see the problem itself."

Patricia Fara

Was it acceptable that he closed the doors on her aspiration to have a child and made her dependent on in vitro fertilization centers and himself? No matter what this was called, engagement or operation, it could not be accepted. "What kind of game is this?" she murmured.

"It is not the world of the good here but the world of those who play well."

Shakespeare

She was also a weakness hunter. She leveraged the weaknesses of others to her advantage. "But I have never imprisoned anyone in the dungeons of his weaknesses," she murmured.

"The worst evil you can do to a person is to imprison him in a hope."

Jean François Lyotard

Galina's pregnancy was already noticeable. She called on her mother, "Mom, can you take a photo of my belly?" "Of course, dear," replied her mom. Galina got the pregnancy test result in one hand, pulled up her blouse and had her picture taken making a victory sign with the other hand. She sent the photo to Doruk.

Doruk was in the field. He saw the message on his phone but decided to check it later. "After all, there is no need to give the impression that I care too much about her," he muttered

He opened the message when he got in the surveillance vehicle. He was shocked when he saw the photo. He started to pant and his whole body started to tremble...

Galina often sent her belly pictures to Doruk. Every time he saw the photos, he pretended to smile even though he was suffering inside. Galina was slowly weaving the spider web from his brain to his heart. She was determined to seize his mind and heart and shatter all his emotions.

"Should I tell Doruk that the child is from him in order to turn him into a better source?" asked Galina to Grigory. Grigory replied, "What if it backfires and he moves away from you?" "I don't think so," said Galina.

A few days later, Grigory called on Galina to come to his room and said, "I thought about your idea. Let's implement it. But be very careful. Also make sure to take a look at Doruk's photo several times a day so that the child may resemble him," and he laughed. Galina started to laugh too. She said, "I'm not sure whether it will work, but let me give it a try." This was kind of a seriocomic joke, for Grigory had not completely disregarded the possibility of Galina's pregnancy being from himself.

Where there is a joke, there is a hidden problem."

Goethe

Galina was sending photos to Doruk almost every day.

Doruk did not know what to do. It was as if he were sleepwalking. He could not get out of the bed in the morning, for he could hardly sleep at night and then he would sleep until noon. His mind was busy with many things every second. He became so absent-minded that he would even forget to take the medicine prescribed by the psychiatrists of the service. In a sense, he was in a state of coma. When he told them that he forgot to take the medicine, the doctors gave him vitamins and informed his supervisor that Doruk needed to be reminded of taking his medicine every day. His colleagues felt sorry for him and never left him alone by planning various events. They became experts on playing dart and bowling, keeping track of the latest movies and finding different venues of entertainment.

While sipping his tea, his supervisor suddenly put the glass on his desk. He seemed to have thought of something. He reached for the phone. "Hello, is Doruk any better? Hmm, no improvement at all? Okay," and he hung up. He took another sip from his tea looking at the window. He picked up the phone again and said, "Could you come to my office?" His supervisor had warned him verbally and in writing time and again, but to no avail.

"How are you?"

"Fine, and you?"

"I'm fine, too. Take a seat."

"Thanks."

"Doruk, life has its ups and downs. Thanks to you, we made the first big blow to the structure of the UN Security Council. Most importantly, they did not understand the blow came from us. They are just looking into it. They have some hunch, but nothing came out of their research.

"Yes."

"Doruk, look, your father entrusted you to us, do I need to tell or repeat this?"

Doruk was silent.

"It isn't even certain that the child is yours. Why did you so quickly give yourself up? If you are going to come to work like this, don't!!! Why should we put you in jeopardy? Punish your success? Are we traitors?"

Doruk was looking down.

"Answer me."

"Definitely not, it didn't even cross my mind. I just can't help thinking whether there had been an accident."

"We told so many times that the injection was effective."

Doruk kept silent.

"Go get your gun and leave it here in this drawer."

"Doruk left the office and returned with his gun. He took the clip out and handed his gun. His supervisor ordered, "the spare clip as well."

Time was moving fast. Doruk noticed for the first time that it moved so fast. He couldn't stop or hold the time. He muttered to himself, "How can one entertain the idea of killing his own child or miscarriage? May God not test anyone with this?"

His supervisor hadn't assigned him a job but office work for months. Doruk showed no sign of improvement. His supervisor had ordered him not to contact Galina in any way other than phone until she gave birth. Despite the order, he proposed to meet with her several times, but Galina was continuously avoiding him making excuses such as feeling sick and nauseous.

The activities with his colleagues no longer entertained him. His friends had listened to Doruk's dream so many times. He was constantly repeating it saying, "There will certainly be a way out. God warns his believers to be prepared by showing them the evil that could potentially happen to them in their dreams." His colleagues were assuring him, "Yes, if God did not wish so, you wouldn't have seen that dream. There is light ahead."

His supervisor called Doruk to his office.

"Look Doruk, here are the information and photos coming from our sources in Moscow." He could see Galina's swollen belly in the photos. Doruk muttered to himself, "It has been over eight months now." His supervisor said, "Look, the man whose hand she is holding in the other photo is an ex-politician. He was removed from the office on the grounds that he was a supporter of EU and USA. He is trying to be re-elected. In short, whether this child from you or from this man is not certain. You know that the Russians usually do not own a child even if the child is theirs. The man is rich and good-looking. It seems the child is from him, so he is enjoying his time with Galina."

Doruk's expression on his face changed in an unrecognizable way. He was quite disturbed both by the probability that the child was not from him and Galina's being with somebody else.

His supervisor continued, "We have a few ideas in mind. There is not much we can do other than waiting and observing. If we try to intervene in Galina's affairs, she might be compromised, and we may not be able to use her again.

A few days passed by. Doruk came to work in a bad mood. He sat down at his desk and picked up the phone. "Chief, are you available?" The supervisor said, "Available on the phone." "Can't we take a DNA sample from the baby in the operating room right after Galina delivers?" asked Doruk. His supervisor said, "Come to my room."

"Doruk, I will immediately ask for information from the sources again and we will keep you posted. This is too risky. The hospital is not the only place where we can get a sample. But if it is a private hospital, that would probably be too difficult."

"Sir, shouldn't we investigate maternity hospitals?"

"We will investigate, don't worry."

"Yes sir, that would be great. If we don't get a DNA sample at the hospital, it may take a few months before we can manage to get one. But..."

"But what? Doruk, should we put Galina and our Moscow team at risk so we can comfort you as soon as possible? Everyone should die, so Doruk can live?!"

"I didn't mean that."

"Be a little patient and you have filed a petition for the terrorism department. Those working for that department stay in prison for years in order to create sources. Why are you so impatient?"

Days had flown by. Doruk was completely messed up.

According to Doruk's estimation, Galina was supposed to give birth around this time.

CHAPTER 4

TEARING DORUK'S HEART OUT

Now Doruk was keeping his distance from his supervisor who had promised to take the baby's DNA sample. Doruk thought he withheld some information. Galina still hadn't replied to him either. Sources in Moscow had informed that the child was born, and that Galina was taking care of the child at her mother's house.

Doruk was mentally exhausted. Neither the personal development books nor the medication he was on was of any help to him.

He sat in front of his computer and decided to search open sources first. At least there had to be something on the internet. He did a search typing Galina Ivanova. None of the information that came up belonged to Galina. He looked through all the media news of the last three months. There were too many people with the same name.

This time he began to search about Denis Zaytsev. He read in the news that Denis's trial had resulted in an acquittal and his reputation had been restored. "It's a very ugly slander," he thought.

He called Oğuz in the evening. They agreed to meet at Tunalı Hilmi Street.

Oğuz asked "Brother, you seem to have lost your joie de vivre entirely, you look so upset... I've been working on Russia for the last few days. It must be because of that."

"What have you been searching for?"

"There is an issue that I came across in the news."

"Bro, do you speak Russian well enough to read the news?"

"I get them translated via a software."

"Is it a useful software?"

"Yes."

"Still, there must be a certain loss in the meaning."

"There is."

"What's the story?"

"They slandered a man claiming he was a child molester."

"Then what happened?"

"The man was acquitted."

"This is usually what happens; when you give the money in Russia, you get acquitted. They just can't resurrect the dead with money, acquittal is a simple thing for them."

"What?"

"Yes, brother, why did you react so much?"

"In such an issue?"

"Yes, it's. In all parts of life, brother; you know, if money gets involved, it has no limits!"

"But if the guy were a celebrity?"

"It does not matter. Bribery dominates the society like metastatic cancer. You know, I lived in Russia for five years."

"But hasn't it been long since you got back? So, it never improved?"

"Yes, time has passed, but it takes at least two generations to change the mental structure there."

*

Doruk went to the famous fish restaurant located on Turan Güneş Street all by himself. He started to drink. The 70 cc raki bottle was about to run out. His face was very pale and everyone in the restaurant was looking at him.

He slowly rose from his seat and murmured to himself, "I've drunk all this?" His eye was on his cell phone at the same time. He was regularly checking it to see if there was a message from Galina. "Oh, I wish I got a message now and I would reply saying, 'If you loved me so much, did you find me worthy of a killer, hysterical bitch like yourself?'" he murmured.

> *"Unexpressed emotions will never die; they are only buried alive and will come forth later in uglier ways."*
>
> **Sigmund Freud**

> *"The majority of hysterical women are extremely attractive, and they are even the most beautiful representation of their sex..."*
>
> **Sigmund Freud**

He left the fish restaurant. The valet fetched his car. He did not forget to tip the valet.

He decided to tour by car. He was driving very fast under the influence of alcohol. "This is the way to drive this car," he muttered.

A few hundred meters away, he saw the emblem of a club across the street. He stopped in front of it. A man with long gray hair opened his door. "Welcome sir," he said. Doruk replied, "Thank you." The man looked like a street valet. He pointed with his hand and said, "This way, please." Doruk began to walk in heavy steps. As he went through the door, a private security guard moved a metal detector over Doruk's body with a smile. Doruk didn't have a gun on him. The security guard pressed on the elevator button. Doruk fixed his eyes on the elevator door as the elevator was coming up. The security guy blinked at the parking assistant and smiled. The parking assistant smiled back and went back out into the street.

Doruk went down two floors in the elevator.

When he walked in, he saw a booth at the entrance with cigarettes, chocolate, teddy bear, duck and roses. He continued to walk slowly. When he entered the club, he saw girls dancing on the dance floor on the left. He was walking so slowly that he drew the attention of all the people inside.

A bald man came up to him and said, "Sir, let me host you in a nice loge." Doruk slowly walked with him without saying anything.

When he got into the loge and sat down, the waiter quickly came and placed a rectangular pillow under his arm. "Thanks," said Doruk. The man who met him at the entrance of the club asked,

"What would you like to drink, sir?"

"Beer is probably the best after raki."

"Do you prefer Miller or Efes?"

"Make it Miller with a slice of lemon."

The man told the waiter aloud, "Go get an ice-cold Miller with lemon and bring five kinds of fruit and pistachios."

The man approached Doruk a little closer and said,

"I am Musa, the headwaiter."

"I'm Doruk."

"Doruk brother, a very nice new dance group has arrived, I can invite the dancers here so you can have a little chat with them."

"Yeah, where are these girls from?"

"They are all from Russia."

"Okay, let them come, but I don't speak Russian."

"Okay, I'll introduce you to the one who speaks Turkish, someone in the group who worked in Turkey before."

"All right."

While Doruk was watching the dance show on the stage, a beautiful tall girl with long blond hair and fair complexion came along with the headwaiter.

"Hi dear, I'm Kristina."

"Hi, I'm Doruk."

"Nice to meet you."

"Where are you from? Nice to meet you too."

"I'm from Kiev."

Doruk raised his hand and gestured to the headwaiter.

"Yes, brother."

Doruk said angrily, "You told me this girl was Russian, but she says she is Ukrainian."

The headwaiter said laughing, "Brother, they used to be a part of Russia during the Soviet Era, that's why."

Doruk also started to laugh, "Well, let's get it this way." Suddenly, it occurred to him that he was laughing for the first time in a long time.

The woman, looking at the headwaiter, asked, "What's up, blad?"

The headwaiter replied, "Nothing."

When he finished his beer, Doruk called on the headwaiter and asked for another one.

In the meantime, the headwaiter approached the table and began to tidy it up.

"OK, don't worry, I'll leave a tip. Don't show off."

"No brother, not for that reason."

"Take a seat for a couple of minutes. Let' me buy you a drink."

"No, brother, I'll drink that water."

"Okay."

"If the girl didn't suit your taste, let me bring another one."

"No need."

"But you don't raise glasses with water...To death... oh, to health..."

"Cheers..."

About an hour had passed by. Doruk was staring at the stage with dull eyes. Then he raised his hand and asked for the bill. He paid it and went out with heavy steps.

When the valet brought his car, he said, "Sir, I can drive you home if you want." Without replying, Doruk sat in the driver's seat, closed the door and shifted the gear to D. He opened the window and handed some coins to the valet.

When he woke up in the morning, he opened his eyes at the hospital.

As he was driving down the protocol road, he hadn't noticed the red light, and a car driven by another intoxicated driver had hit Doruk's car in the side. Doruk had flown out of the right window because he was not wearing his seat belt. There were 15 stitches due to glass cuts and fractures in his arms and shoulders. His brain tomography had also been taken. Gazi University emergency service stated that he should be monitored for twelve hours.

Two Days Later

Doruk was discharged from the hospital and went back to see the psychiatrists of the service. The psychiatrist, Dr. Aybetül asked, "Your colleagues told to your supervisor that you had raised your glass 'to death.' Is that right?"

Doruk did not answer. Then Aybetül continued to speak softly,

"According to Freud, the words that you accidentally and inadvertently say are your repressed desires. It's called 'the Freudian slip.'"

Doruk listened without a reaction.

"You did not consciously commit suicide as a result of your experiences. You tried to do this in your unconscious."

"You were heavily drunk and went out with your car, even though you knew you were going to have alcohol. You refused the valet's offer to drive you home. You drove down the protocol road while you could go home using another road. You drove too fast. There was a desire to die in an accident in your unconscious as you went down to the bridge from that road. Because you knew that if you took the other roads, the car would not accelerate until you dozed off, and that there had previously been fatal accidents, especially on the road curve right before the bridge. You didn't even say 'it won't matter if I die,' but 'Let me die and be saved.'"

Doruk was silent.

"Let's increase the dose of your medication and see what happens, okay? But use it on a regular basis, and I'll see you every week."

"I will."

"You have to walk at least forty-five minutes each day in addition to the medication."

"Got it."

"Other than that, you need a new hobby."

"Hmm…"

"This hobby can be a sports activity."

"For example?"

"For example, you can ride a mountain bike. The bicycles break down constantly. You can buy its spare parts and install and dismantle them."

"Interesting."

"A different world, right? By the way, would you like to talk about your dream which you shared with your colleagues?"

"Yes, that dream is important to me."

"It would be helpful if we investigated the meaning of the dream."

"I think so, too."

"We need to focus on the things that triggered the dream. What had you been thinking about the day before you dreamed, what kind of a day had you had?"

"It was an ordinary day. There wasn't an issue with Galina yet."

"Were you generally concerned and worried?"

"No, I wasn't. I was very happy. I was living a life focused on success in my career."

"Well, can this dream be somehow related to a trauma in your childhood?"

"I don't think there was an incident that had affected me negatively except for my father's martyrdom."

"Then let's not evaluate this dream psychologically."

"What do you mean?"

"You had a messenger dream."

"You mean I had seen some fragments of the future?"

"Well, some clues…"

"So, should I expect to be ascended to heavens now?"

"Can you think about your dream and tell it again?"

"I see myself on a slide."

"You see yourself from the outside?"

"No. I'm sitting on the slide."

"…"

"Then I tilt my head down. The water flows down under me and I'm starting to slide down with this water. Then a woman in black veil slides in front of me. She's got sneakers on her feet. I'm spreading my arms sideways to avoid hitting her. I stop. I don't hit her. Then she falls into the pool. The water rises after she falls into the pool. I'm underwater first. But then the water suddenly lifts and takes me up to the sky. The water is very clear at that time and the color of the sky is something between white and blue."

"What color are the sneakers on the woman's feet?"

"Whitish."

"The black veil is an indicator of distress. So, the woman is underneath as she slides down the slide?"

"Yes."

"This woman is a representation of a problem you will experience with someone lower than your status or under you."

"Hmm, like Galina, because she was doing what I ordered her to do."

"Yes, exactly."

"As a result, we can talk about it even for hours, like the color of your shoes, your being lifted up to the sky and not beyond it."

"…"

"So, according to your dream, you will go through a troubled process and eventually enter into a process that will lead to success. What has happened maybe it will happen again. You must be strong. It will end well."

"I'll try."

"Don't try! Make it happen and be successful."

"Alright."

"Do you want me to give you a hint about these kinds of dreams?"

"Sure."

"Both domestic and foreign sources state that only the chosen people with a pure soul can see messenger dreams so that God sends that person a message."

*

When the weekend arrived, Doruk made an online research to find bicycle companies. He went to the first bicycle dealer he found. The bicycles were all shapes and sizes. Front shock absorber, rear shock absorber, disc brake, V brake, designs made of such metals as aluminum, carbon, chromium etc. Doruk was very surprised when he saw the prices as well. They were quite pricey. An old man came by and asked,

"May I help you?"

"Sure, I'll buy a bike for sportive purposes. What would you recommend for beginners that is of good quality and reasonable price?"

"Look, that model hanging over there is very lightweight and 27-speed, has disc brake, Shimano gear and brake systems on it."

"How about the price?"

"The most affordable model considering the material quality."

"Why is the price affordable?"

"It is from last year and the last one we have."

"Can you give me a discount?"

"The price is as low as it can be because it's on sale, but I can give you a helmet as a complimentary gift."

"Is there an ideal place to ride bikes in Ankara except for Eymir?"

"The most ideal place is the area around Lake Eymir."

"Could you recommend me some magazines and web pages about cycling? I will do it as a hobby so that I can be distracted."

"Of course."

He left the bicycle shop. They were going to deliver the bike to their branch near Lake Eymir. He got in the car and saw a message on his phone. It was from Filiz and it included a photo of a book. "The destination is bookstore," he murmured. He bought the book and started to read it when he got home. As he read it, he highlighted interesting sections and marked certain sentences with stars. It was a very enjoyable book with many analogies and examples.

He finished reading the book in two days. He took a photograph of the "thank you" section at the end of the book and sent it to Filiz. "So, it's over," Filiz wrote back. "I finished it and thank you for suggesting the book to me. If you're not working on Saturday, let's go to Eymir for a bike ride, have a snack, and do the book's critique." Filiz typed, "Sunday 11:00 am. @ Eymir." "See you then," Doruk responded.

The next day in the morning he felt a huge fatigue. He could hardly get out of bed or move his arm. He had never had an energy decrease like this before. It was weird. He couldn't make sense of it. He called his colleagues. He said he felt bad and didn't go to work. "I hope I'll be fine by Sunday," he murmured.

Doruk was at Lake Eymir ten minutes early. He parked his car in the parking lot and went to the shop to get his bike.

"Hi, I'm here to get my bike."

"Of course, you should have a voucher."

"Oh yes, here you are."

"I will keep you waiting for a little bit."

"Sure."

"Would you like some tea?"

"No, thanks."

A few minutes later his bike arrived.

"I've checked the tires and brakes. I hope you enjoy riding it."

"Thanks."

Doruk started to ride his bicycle to the parking lot. He stopped and lifted the seat. "It's okay now," he said.

When he got to the parking lot, he felt the vibration of the phone. "Yes, Ms. Filiz," he said. Filiz sent him her location.

Doruk met Filiz there and they went to the bike shop together to rent a bike for her.

"Shall we go to my car? I forgot the book," said Doruk suddenly. Filiz replied, "Okay."

They took the book from the front seat of the car and proceeded to the forest through the gate where security was located. They slowly started pedaling, chatting and enjoying the nature. It was great that the wind was blowing over the lake, leaving a trace of the delicate touch. "There are some places to sit ahead, let's eat there," he suggested. Filiz replied, "Fine."

They parked their bikes when they approached the restaurant. Doruk pulled out the book from the storage compartment of the bike.

They moved slowly towards the restaurant and ordered their meal.

Tea came in a samovar. Filiz began to talk about herself and the conversation led up to her ex-husband. Doruk was listening and he said, "It's not easy to get to know people, sometimes you think you know them for ten years, but then you experience something, and you say, 'I never got to know them.' This is what life is." Filiz said, "There is nothing so disgusting as being cheated. I do not give by blessing to him. May he not die before he lives the same thing."

Doruk was startled. "Something has just occurred to me. Can I use your phone to go on the internet?" he asked.

"Sure, but why aren't you checking it on your phone?"

"I forgot to plug it in at night and it's about to shut down."

It had occurred to Doruk that somebody might have sent a code to prevent a search about Denis Zaytsev both on his phone and computer. For this reason, he was going to check it on Filiz's phone.

She unlocked the phone and handed it to Doruk. Filiz said, "Let me look at that book in the meantime." Doruk handed the book to her. She started going through the pages.

"Let me take pictures of the parts you've underlined in the book when you're done with the internet," she said.

"Alright," responded Doruk.

While going through the pages, Filiz suddenly said, "Look, this sentence is great; 'Be careful about not what he says, but how and why he says,' and in the next paragraph, the sentence that reads 'they whispered gilded words to deceive ' is great."

"Yeah, I liked it a lot, so I put an exclamation mark next to it".

"I noticed that."

She was glimpsing at Doruk as she went through pages. She noticed that Doruk's color had changed. He blushed and his eyes became wide open.

The news he saw on Google had turned him upside down. A report based on social media reported that politician Denis Zaytsev had married an interpreter named Galina Ivanova. The reader comments were flooded with congratulation messages.

"Oh my God!!! My child is in the same house with this pervert!" Doruk muttered to himself.

www.ingramcontent.com/pod-product-compliance
Lightning Source LLC
Chambersburg PA
CBHW071319130626
46556CB00004B/1655